DOCTOR WHO
BLACK ORCHID

Based on the BBC television series by Terence Dudley by
arrangement with the British Broadcasting Corporation

TERENCE DUDLEY

Number 113 in the
Doctor Who Library

A TARGET BOOK
published by
the Paperback Division of
W.H. ALLEN & Co. PLC

A Target Book
Published in 1987
By the Paperback Division of
W.H. Allen & Co. PLC
44 Hill Street, London W1X 8LB

First published in Great Britain by
W.H. Allen & Co. PLC 1986

The BBC producer of *Black Orchid* was John Nathan-Turner
the director was Ron Jones

Printed and bound in Great Britain by
Anchor Brendon Ltd, Tiptree, Essex

ISBN 0 426 20254 6

Contents

Prologue

The young man in the white jacket was a professional and knew he had very little time left. His right foot kicked back savagely and repeatedly with all his failing strength but, although the heel of his shoe thudded cruelly into his attacker's legs, it did nothing to lessen the grip of the mishapen hands about his throat.

He tore again at the hands with his fingernails but it was in desperation born of despair, for his experience told him that there was no feeling in the brutish hands that were choking him to death. He drove back with his elbows, first one and then the other but again the body of the grunting beast behind him proved impervious. With the singing in his ears he knew he had nothing to lose by attempting a final ruse. Fighting his instinct for self preservation he forced himself to go limp. The trick worked, for a moment later the fearsome hands loosened their grip and the young male nurse allowed himself to slip to the floor at his assailant's feet.

He lay on the floor taking the air into his deprived lungs as silently as possible, thankful for the stertorous, guttural noises coming from his patient. He lay with his eyes open, conscious that the lack of light in the corridor would support his subterfuge, and bit his lip as a well shod foot stirred his oustretched arm before stepping over it. He listened to his patient's unhurried retreat and was tempted to lie where he was until the monster was well clear when he would summon help from the Indian. But as the danger diminished and the singing in his head subsided he remembered he was a professional, and a very highly paid professional at that. Unpleasant though the job was, he considered himself lucky to have it and he would be foolish to throw it away by compounding his carelessness with cowardice. If anyone in the household was harmed through this escape the blame would attach to him. He'd been warned by the Indian never to turn his back when the moon was full, but he had dismissed this as superstitious rubbish. He knew better now. He got cautiously to his feet.

The chapel clock began to strike three.

Ann Talbot stirred as the reverberating bell penetrated her sleep. Her small face, framed by the dark, bobbed hair and washed white by the shafted moonlight, took on a restless, resentful expression. Her slight body twisted in the expansive fourposter bed as if turning from the offending strokes of the relentless hammer.

She never stayed at Cranleigh Hall long enough to become used to the pervasive sound of the chapel clock at night in spite of being given a room as far from the tolling bell as the sprawling Jacobean mansion would allow. Charles said it would be different when they were married and her stays at Cranleigh became longer. He never heard the clock, he said. It had long ago become submerged in that part of his mind reserved for all too familiar sounds.

Ann's fitful sleep was still deep enough to keep from her the small, sharp click that emanated from the panelled wall beside her bed and the controlled, rhythmic, stertorous sound in the void beyond a section of the panelling as it hinged back. There was no further movement for fully a minute during which time the laboured breathing settled to a lengthened rhythm. Then an amorphous shadow detached itself from the black void and eased slowly towards the sleeping girl.

Moonlight filtered to a pair of monstrously deformed hands clasped together in front of the slowly moving shadow. The hands moved up out of the light to a face masked in shadow and the breathing became muffled.

The shape stopped at the edge of the bed and one eye, above the hands, caught a glimmer of light from the distant mullioned window. Narrowed and unwinking the eye fixed upon Ann, taking in her every restless movement. One of the monstrous hands began to inch forward.

A sudden sound from the void at the wall arrested the movement of the hand, and the eye flicked away from Ann, as the figure retreated into deep shadow. The muffled breathing stopped.

The white coat of the male nurse filled the gap in the panelled wall and glared in the revealing moonlight as the young man crept cautiously into the bedroom. He looked cursorily at the girl in the bed and shaded his eyes from the moonlight as he peered round the shadows. He heard the rasp of resumed breathing too late. A crippling blow to the back of his neck robbed him of his legs but a massive strength behind the deformed hands prevented his body from collapsing to the floor. The nurse was borne high to the opening in the panelled wall and on the black side of the partition the breathing became less tortured as the body ceased to be a burden.

The squeal of old hinges was exaggerated in the deep stillness that followed the strident clanging of the chapel clock and Ann came fully awake. She lay rigid for several fearful moments after her mind focussed on the reality of unfamiliar shadows cut sharp by the blades of moonlight. Then she sat up and reached for the bedside lamp. The light, suffused by the silk shade, banished the most frightening of the shadows and softened the edges of her fear. Ann eased herself down from the huge bed and moved like a ghost to the bedroom door. The key appeared to be as she'd left it. Her hand found the door knob. She turned it slowly and gently, and pulled. The door was still locked. She breathed a sigh of relief and went back to bed.

Locking the door had become a habit whenever she stayed at Cranleigh. It helped to get her to sleep, to help her cope with the inevitability of the nightmares she invariably had when she stayed here. Charles laughed at her, not unkindly. She knew he did it to still her anxiety but it was something he couldn't be expected to understand and, like most people faced with something they didn't understand, he was embarrassed and laughed. George was never like that. *He* would have understood. But then she'd never had nightmares at Cranleigh when George was alive. Everybody said that it was the shock of George's death that caused them and that everything would settle down ... settle into place ... in time.

They meant, of course, when she'd had time to forget George. But she knew she would never forget him. She had loved George as she knew she could never love his brother, but this was something Charles *did* understand, or said he did. She would come to love him in time, he said. He would make her love him.

But it was George she saw in those dreams: George dying in that awful Orinoco river; George with those frightful-looking Indians ... the ones with lower lips pushed out with plates ... like platforms ... like ducks ... dreadful! She put out the lamp and lay thinking about the man she had promised to marry, the brother of the man she really loved swallowed forever by the rain forests of South America.

It wasn't until Ann's breathing had settled in sleep that the panelled door moved the last two inches to close with a gentle click.

1

A Doctor to the Rescue

Charles Percival Beauchamp, tenth Marquess of Cranleigh flipped the half-crown into the air and watched it spin in the bright morning sunlight.

'Heads,' said an elegant young man languidly. Both watched the coin fall to the closely-cropped turf, tail side uppermost.

'We'll bat,' decided his lordship as he recovered his coin.

'On that?' questioned the elegant young man not so languidly. He looked out across the trim expanse of cricket field towards the distant strip of sage green at either end of which sets of three stumps stood erect. 'Why don't we delay the start? Give it a chance to dry out a bit.'

'No,' said Lord Cranleigh firmly.

'My lot won't mind if it'll give your chap a chance to get here.'

The young nobleman smiled in acknowledgement of his opponent's sporting offer and looked down at the turf still damp from the light, early morning rain. The surface would favour the fielding side, giving a grip to the ball on the wicket and slowing down the run-rate in the outfield. A delay in starting this annual match with the county side would indeed give more time for his substitute player to arrive from London, but it was an event in support of charity and many of his tenants were engaged in voluntary tasks in a complicated administrative process that would be severely embarrassed by the smallest postponement. He would bat and take his chances. Cricket was more than a game, it was a way of life. And the name of the game was synonymous with integrity.

'Thanks, old man,' murmured Cranleigh, 'but we'll bat.'

He watched the visiting skipper mount the steps to the pavilion with thoughtful eyes and his generous mouth, under the trim fair moustache, drooped a little at the corners now that he was alone. He wondered again what sort of player 'Smutty' had sent in his stead. 'Smutty' Handicombe was one of the finest batsmen of his generation and could have turned out for England if his professional commitments had allowed. It was, one supposed, quite remarkable that this was the first match London's leading brain surgeon was to miss in the last five years. But he'd promised to send a reliable deputy and 'Smutty' was always as good as his word.

The Marquess of Cranleigh tripped lightly up the pavilion steps on his way to the dressing room to change.

The steam locomotive chuffed and clanked its way through the lush Oxfordshire countryside pulling the four coaches into and beyond the small, deserted station. Few trains serviced this line and even fewer stopped at Cranleigh Halt. Trains halted here on request . . . on the request of the handful of local inhabitants who were all known to the drivers and the guards. The station was not staffed. There was no booking office; passengers travelled on trust. In summer a railwayman came from Bicester to tend the tiny garden and in winter a fire was laid in the open grate of the small waiting room but no passenger was ever there long enough to light it. The fire was laid as a courtesy and accepted as such by the tramps – the gentlemen of the road – who reciprocated by keeping their temporary shelter tidy. Cranleigh was a good touch. You could always rely on a generous hand-out from people on this estate. All that was needed was politeness and a tug at the cap.

The train pulled away from the station and chugged into the distance returning barely stirred peace to the foraging birds and the multitudinous insects in the pocket handkerchief garden. The station rejoined the sleeping afternoon. But not for long.

The TARDIS materialised on the eastbound platform.

*

The Doctor and his three companions watched the time rotor settle to a stop and the Doctor activated the scanner. The screen displayed the platform and the warm red brick that surrounded the name, *Cranleigh Halt*. The Doctor patted the console.

'What's the matter, old girl? Why this compulsion for planet Earth?'

'Where?' asked Tegan eagerly.

'Cranleigh Halt?' echoed Adric.

'A railway station,' replied the Doctor.

Tegan prodded Adric out of the way as she moved for a closer look at the scanner.

'That's promising.'

A sigh escaped Nyssa, and Tegan looked at her companion's pretty face, marred by a glum look. 'Cheer up, Nyssa! Your turn will come.' Tegan turned to the Doctor who was adjusting the chronometer and tapping the casing of the tachograph. 'When?'

'Half past one o'clock on June the eleventh, nineteen hundred and twenty-five,' he announced.

It was Tegan's turn to look glum. 'But I haven't been born yet.'

The Doctor looked at her consolingly. 'And no jet lag.' He turned back to the console and thumped the red knob. 'Come on! Let's take a look.'

The Doctor led the way out of the TARDIS and the others followed with a prudence that must have attended disembarkation from the Ark. Which was just as well because the TARDIS had come to Earth very close to the edge of the platform. The Doctor steered Adric from danger with a touch on his arm.

'What's a railway station?' asked the Alzarian.

'A place where one embarks or disembarks from compartments on wheels pulled along those rails by a steam engine.' The Doctor looked along the shimmering rails with nostalgic eyes. 'Rarely on time,' he added.

'What a very silly activity,' said Nyssa with disdain.

The Doctor turned to her with eyes still wistful from looking along the diminishing track of his past, to a time when he, too, was young: a mere five hundred and sixty years. 'Think so?' he murmured. 'There was a time when I wanted to be an engine driver ...'

Tegan smiled. She was the only one of the Doctor's companions who could possibly understand what he was on about.

The Doctor strode down the platform to a gate in a low wood fence passing a number of posters fixed to the station wall. One of these was a picture of an angelic-looking boy dressed in blue and blowing soap bubbles, and another depicted two blissfully happy but badly-dressed children apparently in the act of sniffing at a graphical smell issuing from a tasty-looking meat pie. Adric stopped for a closer look at the pie and Nyssa was checked by his consuming interest.

'What's the matter?'

'I could do with some of that.'

'Some of what?'

'That Bisto,' said a hungry Adric.

The liveried chauffeur had succumbed to the slumbrous warmth of the afternoon and fallen asleep behind the wheel of the imposing Rolls-Royce parked in the station forecourt. He'd forced open heavy lids to watch the twelve-fifteen from Bedford dawdle through the station a quarter of an hour late, but he was waiting for a train coming the other way, the one-twenty from Oxford, and had dozed off again. This was his second call at the station that day. His passenger had not been on the ten-twenty and, since only two trains came through on Saturdays, it would be a poor look out for his Lordship's eleven if his passenger wasn't on this one.

The crunching of feet on the gravel of the forecourt brought the chauffeur fully to his senses. He blinked at the approach of the Doctor and company. He could have sworn the train was going the other way and hadn't stopped. He must have been dreaming. He got quickly out of the car and saluted.

'Good afternoon, sir. I'm Tanner, Lord Cranleigh's chauffeur.'

'Lord Cranleigh?'

'Yes, sir.'

The Doctor always entered warmly into this sort of situation. Mistaken identity it may be, but his insatiable curiosity was aided and abetted by a certain immaturity: that part of the Doctor that had never quite grown up, the part that had wanted to drive a steam engine, the part that sometimes drove Tegan to distraction.

'We're expected?'

Tanner hesitated. He hadn't expected four, and all strangely got up at that. But when was he ever told everything?

'Oh, yes, sir. You *are* the Doctor?'

Tegan frowned, Nyssa pouted, Adric giggled and the Doctor smiled.

'Indeed.'

'Well then, Doctor . . .' Tanner broke off as he glanced past the Doctor at his three companions. He stared hard at Nyssa and the intensity of the disbelieving stare made Nyssa acutely uncomfortable. Had she a smut on her nose, or something?

'May I ask what you're staring at?' she inquired tartly.

It was Tanner's turn to feel embarrassed. There couldn't be two such people so alike in the whole world, but it wasn't his place to tell the young lady that.

'I'm sorry, miss,' he said.

The chauffeur opened a rear door of the Rolls briskly and spoke with respectful urgency. 'Please, Doctor, if you don't mind. The game started on time. His Lordship won the toss and decided to bat first to give you time to get here.'

The Doctor's boundless curiosity crossed fresh frontiers in a rush. Not only, it seemed, was he expected but he was also involved with a game of cricket. He responded with reserve.

'That's very thoughtful of his Lordship.'

'Yes, sir, but I think we should hurry. We took luncheon early . . .' Tanner glanced at the clock in the rose-wood dashboard of the Rolls . . . 'but we will have started again by now. His Lordship's a first class bat but we don't know how

15

strong his support is this year.'

The Doctor reflected that the chauffeur's complete identification with his employer's activities was proof positive that paternal feudalism in England had extended well into the twentieth century. He further pondered that, to many people hereabouts, his Lordship would be known as the master and the thought caused in him a mental wince that returned his attention to the chauffeur's concerned face. The Doctor had been made an offer he couldn't refuse. Mistaken identity notwithstanding, how could he possibly turn his back on a game of cricket?

'Come on, you lot,' he said, 'in you get.'

Nyssa led the way into the Rolls's capacious interior, conscious that the chauffeur was again fixing her with that curious stare. Instinctively she rubbed her hand surreptitiously over her face. The four passengers sank into the luxurious soft leather upholstery as Tanner closed the car door and took his place behind the wheel without once taking his eyes from Nyssa. She turned an anxious face to Tegan.

'What's he staring at?' she muttered.

'Search me,' came the reply from the Bronx via Queensland. The Doctor winced. Tegan picked up the reaction. 'Now what?'

The Doctor turned a pair of mildly enquiring eyebrows.

'Where are we going?' persisted Tegan.

'To a cricket match.'

'Why?'

'Why not?' returned the Doctor blithely. 'And in style too.'

Tegan had no quarrel with that. The aristocrat of automobiles left the station and purred its way through three miles of verdant highways and byways until it reached the gates of Cranleigh Park. The Rolls turned in past the lodge and made its sedate way along the manicured drive for another half mile before the Jacobean pile of Cranleigh Hall came into view.

'What is this place?' Adric wanted to know.

'One of the stately homes of England,' came the Doctor's ready reply.

*

As the driveway forked, Tanner turned the car to the right between low cliffs of rhododendron until the distant cricket field burgeoned. Spectators fringed the field and bunched about the marquee and the pavilion. In spite of the need for haste Tanner brought the Rolls to a dignified halt and left his place to open the door for his passengers.

A figure detached itself from the knot of white-clad players on the pavilion's verandah and hurried towards the car. The Doctor's eyes wandered from the players dotted about the green arena to the scoreboard at the pavilion which telegraphed the grave information that CRANLEIGH XI had scored one hundred and twenty-seven runs for the loss of eight wickets with the last player out for an unlucky thirteen.

Lord Cranleigh broke into a run as a shout from the field and a growl from the crowd signified the near escape of the batsman taking strike. His Lordship greeted the Doctor a little out of breath and with his handsome face flushed.

'There you are, man! Good! I'm Cranleigh. How d'you do? You're just in time. Didn't expect four of...' He trailed off as his eyes settled on Nyssa. 'Good Lord!'

Again Nyssa found herself the object of an intense stare with, this time, Tanner nodding sagely in agreement, for Cranleigh had turned to the chauffeur as if asking for confirmation of something. The nobleman recovered his manners.

'I'm so sorry. Do forgive me staring, but you look exactly like my fiancée. It's quite uncanny.'

Nyssa smiled shyly in relief, smuts and shiny noses banished forever from her mind.

'This is Nyssa,' introduced the Doctor.

'You must meet her,' said Cranleigh, barely acknowledging the name.

'And Tegan and Adric,' went on the Doctor. His lordship took his eyes reluctantly from Nyssa.

'How d'you do?' he greeted them absently. 'You'd better pad up, Doctor. Where's your gear?'

The Doctor shrugged apologetically. 'I regret I have none.'

'No matter. I'll fix you up. We're taking a bit of a thrashing. A hundred and twenty-seven for eight. I made a duck.'

Adric exchanged a look with Nyssa. To them a duck was a web-footed, short-legged, broad-beaked water-bird. Did this activity called cricket include making them in some way?

Cranleigh's eyes had again wandered to Nyssa. He turned to the chauffeur: 'Tanner, take my guests over to the marquee, will you please?'

'Yes, milord.'

Cranleigh took in Nyssa once more. 'I'll join you as soon as I can. Come along, Doctor, I don't want to be pessimistic but I don't think we have a lot of time.'

As if to confirm this a low moan from the spectators succeeded a plangent tock from the centre of the field and Cranleigh hesitated in his stride to watch the ball skied by the striker hovering for a moment before falling into the waiting hands of the fielder in the deep. Cranleigh joined in the applause for the well-held catch and hurried the Doctor onwards towards the pavilion.

'Good man,' murmured the Marquess approvingly of the tenth man in the batting order who was waiting for the dismissed batsman to reach the pavilion before setting out on his journey to the wicket. 'He's giving you time to get the pads on. You're now last man in, I'm afraid. Pity, if you happen to be ...' Cranleigh broke off, not wishing to ask a direct question concerning the replacement's possible prowess. '"Smutty" said he'd send us someone useful with the bat.'

'Smutty?' queried the Doctor.

'"Smutty" Handicombe. Don't you call him "Smutty" at Guys ... at the hospital?'

'No, as a matter of fact,' said the Doctor truthfully.

'Always "Smutty" at school,' murmured Cranleigh before turning to the very serious matter in hand. 'The wicket's still a bit green and the ball's keeping low. The one that got me was unplayable, so watch out.'

'I'll do my best,' promised the Doctor.

In the dressing room Cranleigh briefly introduced those of his side who came readily forward to assist the Doctor accoutre himself in leg pads and batting gloves. The concerned captain of the home side watched his last man in select a bat and make a few promising passes with the left elbow held high. He didn't think, as last man in, that there was much chance, however good this doctor might be, of adding significantly to his side's mediocre score. But he could have another useful talent.

'Any good with the ball?' he asked.

'Not bad,' the Doctor replied with a rare modesty.

'Good! Spin? Medium pace?'

'A seamer. Fast.'

'Top hole!' declared a delighted lord of the British realm.

Tanner had escorted the Doctor's three companions to the hospitality of the marquee where the teams had taken luncheon and where Brewster, the regal butler at the Hall, still supervised his staff in the dispensing of light refreshments. Tegan, to whom the surroundings were comfortingly familiar, had mellowed considerably with her second glass of champagne, while Nyssa sipped a lemonade and looked, with distinct disapproval, on Adric as he unself-consciously wolfed into a plateful of delicately cut smoked salmon and cucumber sandwiches.

'How was that?' came a unified appeal from the centre of the field. The umpire's finger went firmly up in categorical confirmation that the batsman's pad had prevented the ball from squarely hitting the stumps.

'That's you, old man,' announced Cranleigh. 'Good luck!'

'Thank you,' murmured the Doctor and began his purposeful march into the arena to do battle. As he passed the outcoming batsman he nodded at the smile of welcome and encouragement. The Doctor looked over his shoulder for a glimpse at the scoreboard. It read, a hundred and thirty-five runs for nine wickets with the man just out on twenty-four.

Tanner had provided the TARDIS trio with deck chairs and a

privileged position near the pavilion. Tegan and Nyssa watched the Doctor striding towards the pitch as the distant chapel clock struck two.

'Why is it called cricket?' asked Nyssa.

Tegan thought about this. She'd played the game at school and at odd times since without having ever asked that question herself.

'I don't know,' she admitted.

'Oh,' said Nyssa.

Tegan couldn't help feeling a little foolish. Adric came to her rescue by sitting next to her with a plateful of chicken vol-au-vent.

'Really!' exclaimed an outraged Tegan, 'Where are your manners?'

'Manners?' mumbled a masticating Adric. 'What's manners got to do with it?'

The Doctor was taking guard. 'Middle, please,' he requested. The umpire guided a few small movements from the Doctor before signifying that the Doctor was holding his bat directly in front of his middle stump.

'That's middle.'

The Doctor clearly marked the position by scratching a line in the worn turf with his boot and then straightened to look about him, making mental note of the positions of the eleven men in the field.

'Three balls to come,' advised the umpire and moved out of the path of the bowler. The Doctor relaxed his body and gave alert concentration to the onslaught of the ball. It came hurtling in on a good line and length and the Doctor met it firmly in the middle of the bat in a classic forward defensive stroke that broke the tension on Cranleigh's face with a broad smile of approval. He exchanged hopeful glances with the players near him.

'What's the object?' asked Nyssa.

'What object?'

'The object of the game?'

'Oh. The side which gets the most runs wins.'

'What's a run?' mumbled Adric through a mouthful of sticky chicken.

'When the two players run the length of the pitch.'

There was an expectant silence as the bowler commenced his run up to the wicket. He bowled the ball short outside the off stump and the Doctor cut it past point to the boundary. There was enthusiastic applause as the umpire signalled four runs.

'Good shot!' exclaimed Tegan.

'What are they clapping for?' mumbled Adric through lips flecked with pastry.

'Four runs,' said Tegan.

'But they didn't run,' complained Nyssa.

'They don't have to,' explained Tegan, 'if the ball reaches the boundary.'

'What's the boundary?'

'Where the people are.'

'Oh.'

'If the ball's hit over the people's heads that's six runs,' went on Tegan.

'What if it hits the people?' slobbered Adric.

'Nothing. And it doesn't. And do stop scoffing like that!' she added irritably. 'You're making an exhibition of yourself.'

The Doctor glanced the next ball delicately down the leg side and the batsmen crossed for one run.

'Oh, good!' enthused Tegan.

'Good?' said Nyssa curiously.

'Great!' revised Tegan.

'But they only ran once.'

'Yes, but the Doctor's got the bowling.'

'Got the what?'

'It was the last ball.'

'What? Already?'

'Not of the game; of the over.'

'What's an over?'

Tegan's eyes glazed over. She had suddenly become too interested in the game to try to explain its intricacies to the uninitiated. 'You watch a bit of it,' she suggested. 'You'll soon pick it up.'

The Doctor, nicely off the mark and with five runs to his credit, took guard against the spin bowler at the other end. The first delivery was pitched well up to the Doctor who went deftly out to meet the ball in a half volley and drove it high over the sight screen to a concerted murmur of delight and enthusiastic applause.

'There! That's a six,' explained Tegan, joyfully putting her hands together. But Nyssa was feeling excluded by this rather silly game and Adric was content to pursue his gastronomic adventures unhindered by the need to acquire knowledge that held no interest for him.

The spin bowler, out of countenance that a tail-end batsman should treat him with such disrespect, decided to tempt the Doctor away from the crease with a short googly. But the Doctor wasn't deceived by the cunningly concealed action. He saw how the ball left the bowler's hand and knew that when it pitched on the wicket it would turn unexpectedly the other way. Again, with impeccable footwork, he moved with the spin and pulled the ball to the mid-wicket boundary. The Doctor had faced five balls from which he'd scored fifteen runs.

Such was Lord Cranleigh's delight at the prowess of the latecomer he promptly forgot all about his other guests. He moved, in a near trance, to a beautiful woman seated in front of the pavilion whose fine-boned face, shielded by a wide confection of a hat, belied her fifty-five years. The dowager Marchioness of Cranleigh smiled at her son.

'Your substitute is shaping very well, Charles.'

'Isn't he, by Jove!'

The Marquess crouched on his haunches by his mother's deck chair, his eyes alight with admiration. 'If only he could have got here earlier.'

The Doctor watched the bowler direct a fielder to come in closer to the bat, to the silly mid-on position, and smiled. He played the next ball with circumspection; bat together with the pad, and acutely angled to smother the spin and keep the ball well out of the prehensile grasp of the man in the silly position. The fourth ball was a quicker one and short on the leg stump. The Doctor hooked it for six to prolonged applause. The bowler grimaced in self condemnation and sent in another tempter pitched well up on the off stump only to see it cracked through cover to the boundary.

'If only Courtney can keep them out at his end,' muttered Cranleigh, his eyes on the Doctor's partner as the bowler paced in for the last ball of the over. The Doctor punched the ball past the man fielding close in and called 'Come one!' The two batsmen crossed over without attempting another run.

The overjoyed Marquess shot up to his full height like a jack-in-a-box. 'He's going to farm the bowling,' he chortled.

'He's farming the bowling!' squeaked Tegan.

'He's what?' asked Nyssa.

'Farming the bowling.'

'Farming it?' Could this be it, thought Nyssa. The ducks? A duck farm?

'Yes. It means he's going to try to keep the other man ... the one at the other end ... from having to face the ball. The Doctor's the better man but he's the last man in. When either of them is out the innings is over.'

'What do you mean, out?' asked a perplexed Nyssa.

'If the ball hits the wicket ... that's the three sticks ... or if it's caught before it hits the ground, or they could be stumped or run out or leg before wicket.'

'Please!' said Nyssa, shutting her eyes and clenching her fists. 'Please, don't go on!' But Tegan was far too excited to take any notice of the baffled Nyssa.

With total concentration, a fine wit and consummate technical skill the Doctor continued to farm the bowling with a cunning single or an aggressive three runs at the end of every over. The home team's score began to climb spectacularly and the excitement of the spectators mounted with it. Onlookers from all parts of the grounds crowded the ropes and the pavilion and the marquee emptied, something not unnoticed by Adric who took the opportunity further to fortify the inner man.

The Doctor had taken the score from a hundred and thirty-five to an auspicious two hundred and twenty-five when the distant chapel clock clanged the half hour. As the last note sighed into the silence of the still trees surrounding the cricket field, a distinguished-looking man broke from a group of more than usually excited spectators and moved quickly towards the captain of the home team, his piercing eyes ablaze and his hawk-like nose flared; a hunter accepting a challenge.

'Charles!'

'Robert,' responded Cranleigh.

'This man of yours ... !'

'Magnificent, isn't he?'

'Yes,' agreed Sir Robert Muir, 'but d'you know how long he's been out there?'

'About half an hour I should think.'

'Exactly half an hour. He went in at two o'clock.'

'Is something wrong, Robert?' enquired Lady Cranleigh gently.

'Wrong?' echoed Sir Robert.

'You look so upset.'

'Upset,' repeated Sir Robert. 'He's on ninety. Your man's on ninety.'

'Yes, dear,' said Lady Cranleigh. 'We know. Isn't it splendid?'

Sir Robert looked sightlessly at the dowager Marchioness for a moment and then turned again to her son. 'He's five minutes off the record.'

'Record?'

'Percy Fender's.'

'Percy Fender?' questioned Lady Cranleigh.

Sir Robert looked with desolation first at mother then at son, refusing to believe their lack of comprehension. 'P.G.H.Fender,' he explained, 'Captain of Surrey ... made a century in thirty-five minutes. Five years ago. It's the record. A hundred runs in thirty-five minutes. And your man's got five minutes to ...'

He was interrupted by an enthusiastic round of applause as the Doctor stroked a single past cover point and the batsmen exchanged ends at the conclusion of yet another over. Sir Robert took a watch from his waistcoat pocket. 'Is the chapel clock right?' he asked.

'Two minutes slow,' said Lady Cranleigh.

Sir Robert made a mental calculation. 'If he can make nine runs in three and a half minutes he'll have the record.' He watched the players repositioning for the next over keeping the open watch in his hand. And then he saw something that made him speak his anguished thoughts aloud. 'No, no, man! Not now, not now!' The visitors' captain had decided on a change of bowler and he and the new man were in earnest consultation about the placing of the field. As the discussion become protracted Sir Robert's excitement took on frenetic proportions. 'Come on, come on! Get on with it!' he said loudly enough to turn a number of heads. He looked at his watch again and muttered angrily, 'Two and a half minutes. He can't do it!'

The new bowler was of medium pace with a short run up. His first ball was straight and on a good length. The Doctor played it defensively back down the wicket. The bowler fielded the ball and made his way leisurely to his mark. Cranleigh crossed two fingers and Sir Robert began very slightly to twitch. Lady Cranleigh looked at him with raised eyebrows.

'Robert,' she said sweetly, 'if you don't calm down you'll do yourself an injury.'

Sir Robert licked dry lips but didn't take his eyes from the play. The next ball was short outside the off stump and the Doctor drove it through cover for four. He was on ninety-five. The ball had come to the boundary close enough to Sir Robert for him to be tempted to take quick charge of it and throw it in himself. His fever had infected Cranleigh who began himself to vocalise his thoughts. 'Come on, man! A six!'

Lady Cranleigh smiled secretly. What boys they were!

The next ball was again on a length and Cranleigh's prayer was not answered. The Doctor played it coolly with a forward prod. The bowler, conscious that his opponent was within a few runs of his century, was giving nothing away and the next ball was again on a good line and length. The Doctor got forward to the pitch of it and pushed it firmly back to the bowler. Cranleigh looked quickly at Sir Robert who only sensed the move since his eyes were firmly on the field. He flicked a look at his watch and said, 'Less than two minutes.'

'A six, a six,' breathed Cranleigh.

The fifth ball kept dangerously low and turned spitefully rapping the Doctor on the pad. There was a loud appeal, more optimistic than informed, and the umpire was unmoved.

'A minute,' muttered Sir Robert. The bowler started his short run up to deliver the last ball of the over fully intending to frustrate the Doctor's bid for a single run to allow him to change ends. The delivery was straight and on a length but the Doctor leaned back to give himself room and, with a stroke not in the text books, clipped the ball hard past the mid-on fieldsman and began to run. The Doctor's intention was to run three and the batsmen crossed and recrossed. Sir Robert exchanged a look with Cranleigh and put his watch away glumly. 'That's that then,' he said.

The Doctor completed his second run and called again to his partner as the fieldsman got his hand to the ball and turned to throw in. The Doctor had two thirds of the pitch to run and the fieldsman threw hard at the stumps at the bowler's end. The ball sped past the stumps and the Doctor was home. But there was no back up to the throw in and the ball went on through to the boundary.

'Four runs!' gasped Cranleigh incredulously..

'Seven with the overthrow,' almost shouted Sir Robert snatching out his watch. 'He's done it! He must have done it! Yes, he's done it!' He performed a little jig.

'If you start dancing now, Robert,' said Lady Cranleigh smoothly, 'you'll have no energy left for this evening.'

The two men beamed upon her with delight and joined in the prolonged applause that greeted the Doctor's century.

'Will it count, d'you think?' asked Cranleigh.

'What?'

'The record? It's not a first class game.'

'Not a first class game!' expostulated Sir Robert. 'You're playing a minor county side, aren't you? Of course it's a first class game, and of course it counts! I shall report to the MCC immediately.'

'Well,' said Lady Cranleigh rising from her chair, 'I'd

better see how things are getting on at the Hall. Pity Ann didn't feel up to coming. It would have done her the world of good.'

'Ann not well?' asked Sir Robert.

'A headache,' replied Lady Cranleigh. 'She slept badly.' Cranleigh remembered his guests with a pang of guilt and looked hurriedly about him. 'She works too hard,' went on Lady Cranleigh. She's overtired. She'll have to give up all this charity nonsense when you're married, Charles.'

'Yes, mother, of course. But, please! Don't go just yet! There's someone you've simply got to meet, both of you. The Doctor brought some friends with him. Don't go away and I'll find them.' And Cranleigh moved off in search of the Doctor's companions.

Some of Tegan's enthusiasm for the Doctor's prowess at the wicket had infected Nyssa and she too now watched the game with a sense of excitement. Even the replete Adric was showing some interest and both, by now, understood the rudiments of the complicated game and not a little about its niceties. The Doctor continued to dominate the play, conscious that he'd passed his century – though not that he'd beaten a record – and enjoying himself hugely. The umpire called a no-ball and the Doctor lofted it high over the long-on boundary for six.

Tegan was explaining a 'no-ball', with her eyes on the spectator who was obliging by fielding the Doctor's mighty stroke, when her attention was caught by someone moving among the trees that fringed the ground beyond the marquee. She blinked and shielded her sight against the glare of the sun not able, at first, to believe her eyes.

Threading his way through a copse of young beach trees was a man with shoulder-length black hair held in place by a broad yellow head band. He wore a white jacket and baggy white trousers but the really remarkable thing about the man, and something that strained Tegan's belief, was that his lower lip protruded a good four inches beyond his upper lip. His progress through the trees was furtive, something that made his aspect even more sinister. Tegan had vague memories that some tribes of South American Indian so disfigured themselves. She was about to point him out to her companions when Cranleigh called to them.

'Hello, there!'

'Hello.'

'Your friend's doing magnificently.

'Too right,' agreed Tegan. 'He's almost as good as Alan Border,' she added, forgetting in her enthusiasm that neither she, nor the Australian Test captain, had been born yet.

'Who?'

'An Australian I know,' said Tegan demurely.

'Ah! D'you know he's broken the record time for the century?'

'He has?'

'Indeed he has. He's beaten thirty-five minutes set by the captain of Surrey five years ago.'

'Wow!' Tegan was so impressed her mind emptied of the strange figure she'd seen in the trees.

'I'd like you all to come and meet my mother,' said his lordship with his eyes firmly on Nyssa. 'Do you mind?'

He guided the Doctor's three companions towards the pavilion where Lady Cranleigh and Sir Robert were joining in the applause for yet another fine stroke from the hero of the day. 'Mother, may I introduce Tegan and Adric?'

Lady Cranleigh smiled a polite welcome with her mind on the preparations she should be superintending at the Hall. 'How d'you do?' she said, and then, 'What enchanting names!'

Nyssa was a little hidden behind the taller Tegan and Cranleigh encouraged her forward. 'And this is Nyssa,' he said.

He looked searchingly at his mother and wasn't disappointed at the expected flutter of astonishment. The poised dowager Marchioness was caught quite off balance, thinking for a moment she was the victim of a practical joke. Then her wide eyes took in Nyssa's tumbled, shoulder-length hair. 'Tegan, Nyssa and Adric are friends of the Doctor,' explained her son delightedly.

'How extraordinary!' gasped Lady Cranleigh.

'Isn't it?'

Sudden realisation came to the startled woman and she looked at the equally fascinated Sir Robert as if seeking support.

'Worcestershire!' she offered by way of explanation. 'Nyssa, did you say?'

'Yes,' said her son.

'Nyssa Talbot?'

'Just Nyssa, actually,' said her son who had pursued that possible explanation earlier.

'Just Nyssa?' echoed the lady of the manor. She looked directly, almost accusingly, at the increasingly embarrassed girl. 'I beg your pardon, my dear, you *must* be a Worcestershire Talbot.'

'No,' said Nyssa, 'I don't even know what that is.'

Lady Cranleigh again looked at Sir Robert for help. 'Robert?'

'Uncanny,' volunteered the mesmerised knight. 'Quite uncanny.'

'Two peas in a pod,' announced Lady Cranleigh emphatically, 'positively two peas in a pod.'

Nyssa looked in mounting desperation at Tegan who smiled back at her limply. So, Nyssa looked like somebody else. Big deal! Lady Cranleigh's sense of shock subsided enough for her suddenly to become conscious of Nyssa's embarrassment and she was overcome with contrition. 'My dear, you must forgive a pardonable curiosity. Where *are* you from?'

Nyssa looked her inquisitor straight in the eye and, without batting a lid, said, 'The Empire of Traken.'

The dowager Marchioness was clearly impressed by the answer which had a reassuring imperial ring to it, but she was far too well bred to indulge her curiosity further. She allowed herself to be diverted by the Doctor once more middling the ball to the boundary. She joined the applause and then excused herself graciously. Acknowledging salutations from her tenants she made her way towards the Hall.

In the shadow of the bordering trees the Indian with the grotesquely extended lip stood very still and watched her progress.

2

Nyssa Times Two

With the home side's score at two hundred and sixty-three the inevitable happened. Fortune certainly favours the brave but it's also certain that fate can be tempted once too often. The Doctor's luck ran out – literally. In another end-of-the-over scamper to capture the bowling, the stumps were shattered by a brilliant throw in by the visiting skipper with the Doctor two yards from the crease and two runs short of his hundred and fifty.

The pitch was immediately invaded, with a host of cheering small boys well to the fore. Congratulations were showered upon the Doctor from all sides for, by now, word of his record-breaking century had spread far from the cricket field to the four corners of the estate. The Doctor modestly fought his way to the pavilion where Cranleigh, beaming from ear to ear, wrung him by the hand.

'Ripping performance, old man! Allow me to introduce Sir Robert Muir, the Lord Lieutenant of the county.'

'First rate, sir! First rate!' enthused Sir Robert. 'A superb innings! Never seen anything like it. I doubt the master could have done better.'

The good Doctor hiccoughed in the middle of a self-deprecatory murmur, unable to believe his ears. 'The Master?'

'The other Doctor – W.G. Grace.'

Relief assuaged the Doctor's shock as he remembered the legendary leviathan of that name who had dominated the game a generation earlier.

'Oh, yes! Of course! Thank you.'

The Doctor's companions succeeded eventually in penetrating the laudatory crowd surrounding the hero to add their congratulations. Both Nyssa and Adric announced themselves warm converts to a game they had found incomprehensible an hour earlier and Tegan, who had never seen the Doctor engage in her national sport, smiled upon him with a face that worshipped. The Doctor was quite embarrassed.

'That's more like a score,' said his lordship gratefully with a glance at the board. Secretly, he was equally grateful that 'Smutty' Handicombe had been detained by that emergency operation in London. He'd seen 'Smutty' in spectacular form with the bat many times but nothing to equal this. Dare he hope the man was half as good with the ball? He was soon to find out.

When the home side took the field, Cranleigh resisted the strong temptation to open his attack with the Doctor for fear of being thought ostentatious, such was his instinct that he had an all-rounder of rare talent in his side. At the tea interval the county eleven had made fifty-six runs without loss and had clearly taken charge of the bowling. When play resumed Cranleigh tossed the ball to the Doctor and, in consultation, set an aggressive field with three slips and a short leg. The county's stylish number one was lucky to survive the Doctor's opening delivery which, on a sizzling line and length, beat the bat and must have grazed the off stump. The batsman looked so shattered that his lordship had to call upon all his willpower to stop himself smiling. But the partisan audience had no such inhibition and a concerted gasp developed into warm applause. The shaken batsman prodded respectfully at the Doctor's next three deliveries but failed abysmally to keep out the fifth ball which flattened his middle stump.

Lord Cranleigh joined in the rapturous ovation and ran to join the handwringing, back-slapping circle that enclosed the flushed Doctor.

'Where on Earth have you been hiding yourself, man?' he chortled. 'What side do you normally turn out for? Not Guys' Hospital, surely?'

The Doctor smiled inwardly at the adverb, aware that his curiosity and love of the game had, at last, led to the very edge of dangerous ground.

'If you don't mind, Lord Cranleigh,' he said, 'I think it would be better if I remained incognito.' His Lordship was immediately contrite.

'Of course, my dear fellow! Of course!

The captain of the county side, batting number three and no longer languid, came out to the crease determined to put a stop to this nonsense. Dammit, the man wasn't even properly dressed. He took guard and stood erect to take stock of the field, exchanging a tight smile with the man positioned at short leg just four yards behind him. The Doctor's last delivery was on a length and came back off the seam. The determined nonsense-stopper was forced to play at the ball giving an easy catch to the man at short leg whose tight smile relaxed in triumph as the batsman made his way, as languidly as he was able, back whence he'd come amid great whoops of joy from the onlookers.

Cranleigh had inherited the traditional good manners that forbade expressions of jubilation at an opponent's defeat. Not so Tegan. She began jumping up and down to the amazed amusement of Nyssa and Adric.

'He's on a hat trick! He's on a hat trick!'

Nyssa and Adric exchanged a look. Hat trick? And the Doctor not even wearing his hat? Tegan saw their incomprehension not without a little irritation, knowing that she had to embark again on an explanation of what everybody else present knew as a matter of course. She explained patiently that the Doctor had taken two wickets with two consecutive balls and that if he took a wicket with the first ball of his next over he would have made a hat trick. Nyssa looked troubled; Adric positively unhappy. Tegan sighed: 'If you get three wickets with three consecutive balls you get a hat trick.'

'Is that good?' asked Nyssa.

'Of course it's good!'

'How many runs does it score?' asked Adric.

'It doesn't get any runs.'

'Then what *does* it do?' persisted Nyssa.

'It doesn't do anything.'

'But you said it was good,' blurted Adric.

Tegan puffed out her cheeks and clenched her hands, resenting bitterly the diminution of her joy at the Doctor's achievement. 'It's the honour,' she said peevishly.

'The honour,' echoed Adric.

Tegan waved her hands about, mistrustful of words to communicate the depth of her feelings. 'Yes. The honour. The cleverness.'

'Oh,' said Nyssa flatly.

Tegan fumed.

The next over was delayed because the new batsman was late getting to the crease. Number four in the batting order had been taken completely by surprise at the unprecedented dismissal of his captain with a single delivery and had to panic himself into his pads. The field buzzed with excited anticipation as busily as a hive of honey-bees working a single flower bed.

The news of the Doctor's phenomenal performance had penetrated the Hall and one after another of the staff of servants gathered together on the terrace for a glimpse of the distant game.

None of them there assembled saw the Indian break from the cover of the trees and run to the north side of the Hall, the side that gave access to the servants' quarters. He let himself in by a basement door at the foot of mildewed stone steps and made his stealthy way to the back stairs. He climbed carefully to the third floor and padded his way noiselessly down deserted corridors in a methodical but covert search of all the rooms.

The bowler who shared the attack with the Doctor completed his over in a taut hush of expectation. The fact that seventeen runs had been scored from it was treated almost as an irrelevance. The new batsman, who during that over had got off the mark at the first ball and subsequently hit two comfortable and elegant-looking boundaries, now faced the Doctor. The proverbial pin could have been heard to drop on grass in the silence that heralded the Doctor's run up. The anxious batsman distributed his weight evenly and watched the ball in the Doctor's hand with devotional concentration. The Doctor dug the ball in and it rose sharply. The batsman straightened and attempted to pull his bat away to no avail. The ball touched the inside edge of the bat and smacked into the wicket keeper's gloves. The instant appeal was echoed by a good proportion of the onlookers and the umpire's finger went unhesitatingly up. The Doctor had made his hat trick.

The spectators applauded ecstatically. Tegan yelled, 'Good on you, Doc!' and flung her arms around a startled Nyssa. Lord Cranleigh was overcome by the Doctor's success and his joy knew no bounds at the quality of the day's entertainment. Sir Robert declared that this performance could have no equal in the annals of first class or club cricket and resolved to telephone the Marylebone Cricket Club at the earliest opportunity and to delve deeply into Wisden's Almanac – the Bible of the game.

The Doctor's over was responsible for yet another wicket and the rot rapidly set in as the morale of the visitors deteriorated during what remained of their innings.

The Indian had worked his clandestine way to the first floor and the family bedrooms. His stealthy passage down the long corridor was suddenly halted by the sound of a door handle turning. He slipped unhurriedly into the shadow of a large pedestal as Lady Cranleigh came from Ann's room attended my a maid. He watched the two women move to the staircase and begin to descend. He followed at a careful distance.

The larger part of the Hall's staff from the butler and his housekeeper wife to the fourth footman was still crowded onto the terrace. Even Lord Cranleigh's valet was there, clothes brush in hand. From the drawing room Lady Cranleigh looked out on her assembled servants with amused tolerance and, not wanting to interrupt and cause embarrassment, sent her maid with a message for the butler before consulting the clock in the hallway. She was watched by the Indian from the shadows in the curve of the stairs.

Out on the terrace the butler sent his staff about their respective duties before going in search of his employer.

Under the eyes of the watching Indian, the dowager Marchioness, accompanied by the butler, went out onto the terrace to inspect the layout of the running buffet that was to be part of the evening's entertainment. The Indian waited patiently, listening to the distantly heard instructions. Then he heard Lady Cranleigh recross the drawing room. The moment he had been waiting for had come. He would pounce the moment she reached the stairs. But his intention was to be suddenly and unexpectedly thwarted.

As her Ladyship entered the hallway a great shout went up from the distant cricket field, greeting the end of the game and the home side's resounding victory. Lady Cranleigh turned back to rejoin the butler on the terrace, since catering for the continuation of the entertainment was now imminent.

The Indian left the shadow of the staircase and slipped quietly into the passage that led to the west side of the Hall.

The tenants on the Cranleigh estate were reluctant to disperse, all anxious for a closer, longer look at the hero of the day. The Doctor's companions, together with Lord Cranleigh and Sir Robert, had to force a way to the besieged Time Lord.

'An absolutely ripping performance,' pronounced Cranleigh. 'You must come and meet the mater.' To a prolonged chorus of unstinted tribute the Marquess led the way towards the distant Hall.

High up on the west side of the manor house the Indian watched through a barred window the departing tenants and the approaching cricketers. He turned and looked thoughtfully about the room as if seeking a clue, an answer to a great problem. The room was large and agreeable and luxuriously furnished. There was a magnificent bed and deep, comfortable armchairs. A large, handsome desk and a Jacobean dining table and chairs were among the many pieces that spoke of every convenience for gracious living. Bookshelves lined the walls, and where there were no books the spaces were filled by framed flower prints and photographs of exotic plant life. The two discordant notes were the bars on the window and the heavy, dominant door which stood open to reveal a stark passage of unrelieved gloom. The Indian took one more troubled look round the room and then went out to the passage leaving the door open behind him.

On the way to the Hall Tegan fell in beside the Doctor who looked away in embarrassment from eyes still shining with admiration.

'I'd no idea you could play the game like that.'

'I had a bit of luck,' mumbled the Doctor modestly.

'Are you sure you haven't got any Australian blood in you somewhere?'

The Doctor grinned. The idea of a Time Lord possessing, to any degree, a form of blood to which could be attributed human fame or blame was a concept beyond the grasp of the primitive Tegan. 'Quite sure,' he twinkled. 'But I learned the rudiments of the game in Australia.'

'I knew it!' chirped a triumphant Tegan.

The Doctor looked about him to confirm no one was within earshot. 'It was during a previous regeneration. I'd dropped in to intercede on behalf of a group of aborigines. I met a boy called Don. Come to think of it he'd be about the same age now; it was during the mid nineteen-twenties. He had a very good eye. He used to practice hitting a golf ball against a wall with a piece of thin piping. Taught me all I know. I sometimes wonder what may have happened to him, but I always forget to look it up.'

'Wouldn't be Don Bradman by any chance?' said a self-satisfied Tegan.

'That's it ... Bradman. Don Bradman.'

'*Sir* Donald Bradman, that's what happened to him.'

'You don't say?' said the pleased Doctor.

'But I *do* say!'

Lady Cranleigh came from the hall to greet the two teams. 'I hear you've had some splendid cricket.'

'Phenomenal!' said Cranleigh. 'Mother, may I present the

36

Doctor?'

'How d'you do?' greeted the dowager Marchioness.

'How d'you do?' responded the Doctor.

'Doctor who?'

'I'm sorry mother, he'd like to remain incognito. And I think we should respect that after what he's done today.'

'But, of course. But I can't promise I won't be very curious this evening.'

'This evening?' enquired the Doctor politely.

'At the ball.'

'It's fancy dress, isn't it?' asked Tegan.

'Yes, my dear.'

'I thought so. I saw one of your guests arriving. Got up like an Indian with one of those funny lips ...' she gestured appropriately ' ... you know?'

A look flickered between mother and son. 'Really,' said Lady Cranleigh steadily. 'I'm glad you all came prepared.'

Tegan looked puzzled and Lady Cranleigh continued. 'And I must congratulate you on the originality of your costumes. They really are quite enchanting.'

The Time-travellers looked a little self-conscious. The Doctor smiled one of his broad, masking smiles, Nyssa looked down at her knickerbockers, Adric glanced at the star fixed to his tunic, and Tegan grinned at the thought of her Air Australian uniform being mistaken for fancy dress. Lady Cranleigh smiled radiantly upon the Doctor. 'And your costume, Doctor? What's that to be?'

'I fear I brought no fancy dress,' confessed the Doctor.

'In that case I'm sure Charles will be able to fix you up, won't you, Charles?'

'Oh, yes,' agreed Cranleigh. 'We have any number. Quite a choice. We have a museum room. It's a sort of play room my brother and I used to use. Dressing up ... theatricals and all that sort of thing, don't you know. I'm sure we can find you something.'

'In that case,' put in Nyssa, 'I'm a bit hot in this.'

Tegan thought she'd help out. 'And I don't think that any of us can hold a candle to your Indian gentleman.'

Lady Cranleigh again exchanged a private look with her

37

son. 'Charles?'

'Leave it to me,' said his Lordship. 'But first, some refreshment. We have a lot of thirsty players here.'

The statement was greeted by a happy murmur of agreement from those who had laboured in the warm afternoon sun. Cranleigh looked with proprietorial concern on the star of the day's cricket. 'I'm sure the Doctor would like to take a cocktail to his bath.'

'Thank you,' responded that worthy. 'A cool drink would be very welcome.'

'Then come along!' The young nobleman led the way into the Hall. Yet again a look between Nyssa and Adric exchanged their amused puzzlement. Adric had in his mind's eye a complex notion of a bird's rear feathers stuck into a cake of soap. 'What do you do with a cocktail in a bath?' he spluttered.

Lord Cranleigh turned back to look at him with a smile that attributed such ignorance to tender years. 'Drink it, my young friend.'

Adric grimaced and gave up. Cranleigh followed his mother into the drawing room and said quietly, 'How's Ann?'

'Much better for her rest. She's up and about and should be on her way down.'

'Oh, good!'

At a table bedecked with a rich array of bottles and buckets of ice, the butler supported by two footmen and two maids, was preparing to disperse a variety of mixed spirituous drinks known as 'cocktails' that had become fashionable in the United States and had, inevitably, found their way into the homes of the smart set in Britain. The popularity of the cocktail was owed, in no small part, to a flirtation with a mild form of socially acceptable wickedness. The prohibition of alcohol in the States six years earlier had led to secret drinking and the need to disguise the nature of the alcohol that was consumed in public. What had mystified Adric also confused the law enforcement officers in the States. What looked like an innocuous glass of fruit juice could be a concoction based on the alcohol requirement of an individual taste. In Britain, where no such repressive law existed, there was no consequential abuse of alcohol and the cocktail had become little more than a graceful and exotic aperitif.

The spacious room was by no means crowded with the presence of two teams of white-flanneled gladiators and their immediate supporters. Cranleigh gestured towards the range of tall windows. 'When the weather's fine we hold the ball on the terrace. We so enjoy the light, summer evenings. And my mother casts spells on the weather.'

'Charles,' murmured his mother in mild reproof.

'Lady Cranleigh is clearly a bewitching lady,' declared the Doctor in his best Edwardian manner. Her Ladyship glowed. The talents of this engaging young man manifestly extended beyond the cricket field. 'Where have you been hiding this young man, Charles? In future I shall expect to see much more of him.'

Tegan studied the radiant features of their hostess. It was such a great pleasure to be associated with someone like the Doctor when he was displaying the refinement of his social accomplishments. She remembered the time when she was suspicious of his impeccable manners. She had grown so used to so many rough diamonds in her own country. Diamonds without a doubt but, oh, sometimes so in need of a bit of polish.

Cranleigh delighted in his mother's approval of their guest. 'I'll give you a fixture list, Doctor,' he said. 'You must let me know when you may be able to play again. And I can't wait to talk to "Smutty", I can tell you.'

'There's more to life than cricket, Charles,' said his mother dryly. The Doctor was grateful for any dampener to delay the inevitable talk with 'Smutty' that would certainly mean involved explanations complicated by the compelling need to speak the truth. The Doctor reflected, yet again, that curiosity was not without its dangers. It even killed cats, and cats had nine lives. And the Doctor's life was about to become more complicated than any projection of his wildest dreams.

The murmur of polite conversation was suddenly hushed by the appearance of Ann Talbot. The groups of cricketers parted for her as she made her way towards her fiancée and, in her wake, the silence was broken by muted expressions of wonderment. For, seen together, Nyssa and Ann were indistinguishable except in that they wore different clothes and different hair styles. Nyssa's tumbled locks contrasted sharply with Ann's bobbed hair. And Ann's simple white silk dress amply excused Lady Cranleigh in mistaking Nyssa's plum-coloured velvet costume for fancy dress.

The Doctor was startled into expressing on oath. 'Great Gallifrey!'

Cranleigh left his mother's side. 'Ann, my dear, come and meet the hero of the day and his friends.' He brought her forward to Nyssa and the two girls stared at each other, aghast.

Tegan sneaked an astonished glance at Adric and hissed at him, 'Stop it! You're mouth's open.'

'Ann Talbot, my fiancée. This is Nyssa.'

The two girls reached slowly for each other's hands, scarcely able to believe their eyes. Cranleigh went on with the introductions, enjoying for the second time that day the amazement on the faces about him. 'And this is the Doctor.' But Ann was unable to take her eyes from Nyssa. 'And this is Tegan ... and Adric.'

'It's open again,' muttered Tegan out of the side of her mouth. But Adric didn't hear her. Fascination had taken possession of him.

'How d'you do?' said Ann to Nyssa.

'How d'you do?' said Nyssa to Ann.

'Quite fantastic,' breathed the Doctor. 'Even the voices are alike.'

'Worcestershire!' said Ann suddenly. 'Have you an Uncle Percy?'

'No,' replied Nyssa.

Lady Cranleigh shook her head almost sadly. 'Not a Worcestershire Talbot.'

Ann's astonishment beckoned beyond her manners. 'Then where *are* you from?'

'Traken,' admitted Nyssa, trying hard not to make it sound apologetic.'

'Where's that?'

Nyssa looked desperately at the Doctor, who, for some

reason unknown even to himself, looked at the languid young man, who, as captain of the opposing team, had been the centre piece of his hat trick. The languid young man was disposed to attempt to reclaim some of his damaged reputation by suggesting he was something of a topographer. 'Near Esher, isn't it?' he ventured.

The need for a denial from Nyssa was prevented by the arrival of a footman bearing a cocktail on a tray which he offered to the dowager Marchioness.

'Could there be Talbots near Esher?' queried Ann.

'Not possible,' pronounced Lady Cranleigh taking her drink. 'The hunt isn't good enough.'

Tegan marvelled at the question and the answer pointing, as they did, to the divine right by which certain families claimed areas of the country for themselves as if they were otherwise uninhabited. She smiled secretly at the thought of Talbots in Tibooburra, or Thargomindah, or even in Alice Springs.

Cranleigh turned to the Doctor. 'What may I offer you, Doctor? Brewster can make absolutely anything – quite superbly.'

The Doctor allowed his eyes to stray to the large number of bottles representing the wide choice of slow poison readily available. 'I have a tremendous thirst,' he confessed. 'Perhaps a lemonade with lots of ice.'

His Lordship nodded unhesitatingly at his butler. 'Ann?'

'The same as the Doctor, please.'

Cranleigh turned to Tegan. 'My dear?'

Tegan, after tustling with the events of a turbulent day, felt the need for something to settle her down, some relaxing of tension that could be achieved by the decorous imbibing of a modest vodka and orange juice. 'A small screwdriver, please.'

Brewster nodded and Adric blinked. 'Is that something you can drink?' he whispered. Tegan had had more than enough of explaining the inexplicable to Adric. 'Do stop asking silly questions!' she hissed. 'And if only you knew how stupid you look with your mouth like that.'

Adric closed his mouth, looking a little hurt.

Cranleigh had moved to Nyssa who had decided that what

was good enough for Tegan would be good enough for her. 'Thank you. I'll have the same.'

'The same as me, that is,' interjected the Doctor. 'And I'm sure Adric would like a lemonade too.' Neither Nyssa nor Adric was really conscious of the Doctor's intercession, both being totally absorbed by Nyssa's double.

As Cranleigh consulted with his mother about what rooms should be put at the disposal of his four unexpected guests Tegan's interest was caught by a glass display cabinet on a side table which appeared to contain a bloom of some sort. She and the Doctor moved to take a closer look. The cabinet housed an enormous orchid that measured perhaps ten or twelve inches from the tip of one lateral sepal to the other. The lateral sepals and the dorsal sepal were a velvet black while the lowest past of the bloom, the lip, was of the purest gold. Tegan was moved by the sensual beauty of the flower.

'Oh, that's quite beautiful,' she murmured. 'It's an orchid, surely?'

'Yes,' confirmed the Doctor.'

'It looks alive, but it can't be, can it?'

'No. It's been treated. A sort of embalming process.'

After expressing as much curiosity about Nyssa's trouser suit as good manners permitted, Ann returned to the question of her double's habitat.

'Are you really from Esher?'

Nyssa turned tormented eyes to Adric but there was no help forthcoming from that quarter. Adric was busy mentally phrasing his own answer to the inevitable question about his origins.

'I don't even know where Esher is,' said Nyssa glumly. She was rescued from her persistent double by Sir Robert Muir joining them, Tom Collins cocktail in hand, to extol the Doctor's prowess with bat and ball for the benefit of Ann who had been prevented from witnessing the unparalled performance.

Tegan turned at the approach of Lady Cranleigh.

'I was just saying how beautiful this is,' she said, indicating the beautiful black orchid.

'Yes,' agreed Lady Cranleigh.

Tegan looked again at the orchid. 'I've never seen anything like it before. Where does it come from?'

'It was found by my elder son on the banks of the Orinoco.'

'Oh,' responded Tegan, a little intimidated for not being sure what – or where – the Orinoco was.

'A river in Venezuela.' contributed the Doctor helpfully.

'He was a botanist,' went on Lady Cranleigh. 'He wrote a book about his journey up the Amazon and the Negro, and crossing into Venezuela.'

'Of course,' said the Doctor suddenly, 'George Beauchamp, the explorer.'

'Yes,' said Lady Cranleigh sadly. Her hand rested on the glass cabinet. 'And like all explorers he had to go back. This held such a strong fascination for him that he went back two years ago and never returned. It was as if the flower called to him. The natives hold it to be sacred.'

'I'm sorry,' said Tegan softly.

'He had a strong sense of destiny,' said Lady Cranleigh proudly. 'The father of the first Marquess was with Sir Walter Raleigh on his last expedition . . . to the Orinoco.'

She moved back towards the centre of the room looking at one of the many portraits that hung from the walls depicting the succession of Marquesses from the turn of the sixteenth century. The last in the line was of a seated young man bearing an expected resemblance to his bother. George Beauchamp, ninth Marquess of Cranleigh, smiled down on the assembled company with benign approval. Lady Cranleigh smiled back.

'Miss Talbot was engaged to be married to him. But I'm delighted to be able to say we're still to have her in the family.'

Sir Robert looked from Ann to Nyssa and back again. 'That's if Charles marries the right girl. He could be forgiven for mistaking Nyssa for Ann.'

There was a polite ripple of amusement in which all within earshot joined and it prompted Ann's persistence.

'Nyssa what?'

'Just Nyssa.'

'But you can't be.'

'I am.'

A frustrated Ann faced Lady Cranleigh. 'And Nyssa doesn't even know where Esher is.'

'Which shows very good taste,' announced her Ladyship. 'Never mind, Nyssa. You must forgive our vulgar curiosity. And it's high time we all thought about changing.'

'And some of us haven't anything to change into,' Cranleigh reminded himself. 'Ann, come with me! You shall choose something for the ladies and I . . . the gentlemen . . . if everyone will excuse us.'

The two of them departed on their errand while Lady Cranleigh instructed a footman and a maid to show her guests to their rooms. Tegan put down her drink from which she'd taken but a sip.

'No, my dear,' said her Ladyship. 'You finish that. And there's no hurry.' She indicated the young maidservant distributing drinks to other guests. 'Joyce will know when you're ready.'

Tegan picked up her glass, marvelling at the thought that here was a girl younger than she who was expected to anticipate her every whim. If these were the good old days, she thought, it was certainly all right for some. And then she remembered that exactly the same was expected of her on her aircraft. What's changed, she had to ask herself.

Cranleigh opened the door into the attic and switched on the overhead light. Ann followed him into the long, low room circumspectly. She shivered.

'Not cold?' asked Cranleigh solicitously.

'Spooky. Didn't you hear it?'

'What?'

'I thought I heard something move over there.'

'Nothing to worry about,' said Cranleigh.

'Rats?'

'Not up here. Probably a squirrel. Nothing to worry about. Come on!' He led the way further into the attic and leaned to switch on more light. Ann followed warily through the paraphernalia that bridged more than three centuries. There were many costumes, male and female, on frames and protected by dust sheets. There were wigs on blocks, weapons of all kinds, footwear that included high Jacobean boots, saddlery of every sort and innumerable chests and baskets.

'Haven't been up here for years,' said Cranleigh. 'Look at that! Isn't it marvellous?' He was pointing at a suit of armour that was massive and, in some areas, incomplete. 'It's got some pieces missing, or we'd find a place for it downstairs.'

Ann looked at the armour with misgiving. There was something about it that chilled her. She took in the domed skull and the many perforations in the visor which seemed to her like tiny, sightless eyes that, nevertheless, watched her relentlessly. The pauldrons and the breastplate were powerful while the tasset must have protected giant thighs.

'It's Greenwich armour,' said Cranleigh. 'Made in a workshop at Greenwich founded by Henry the Eighth. It was at a time when German armour became fashionable. That was made by a man called William Pickering in 1618 for the first Marquess.'

'Be a bit big for you,' giggled Ann nervously.

'Yes,' agreed Cranleigh. 'And I wouldn't want my head cut off either.' He pointed to an effigy of an executioner that stood close to the armour. The figure stood with legs apart and with arms, that developed from wide shoulders, joined across the chest and suspended over a point where once must have stood the long handle of an axe. Its head and face were hidden completely by a black triangular mask that depended from a skull cap. Ann shivered again.

'Charles, I don't like it here.'

'All right, my dear, we're going. In this chest, if I'm not mistaken, and in that one.'

Ann lifted the lid of a chest and looked at the contents that were carefully folded and interleaved with tissue paper. Cranleigh had, in the meantime, opened a large skip to take out a long, one-piece costume resembling a French circus clown. With it went a complete head covering attached to a chalk-white mask painted to represent a face.

'Here,' said Cranleigh, donning the mask, 'what about this? Pierrot. And I think I remember a Pierrette.' He rummaged further before suddenly hit with an idea. 'Of

45

course! Ann! In that one.' He pointed at a smaller basket. 'Identical costumes. Made for Great-Aunt Arabella and her twin sister. It was for a pageant. Fireflies or beetles or something. They would do nicely for Tegan and Nyssa.'

Ann took a cardboard box from the basket and opened it. From it she lifted a midnight blue tulle dress and a fitted cap and mask from which protruded two long antennae. 'I've got a much better idea,' she said. Setting aside the dress in the box she searched deeper within the basket.

Meanwhile, Cranleigh had added a mid-seventeeth-century Commonwealth costume to that of the Pierrot. Ann picked out an elf-like taffeta dress in laminations of different colours. 'Tegan shall have this,' she said happily.

'Time to go then,' said Cranleigh. They made their way with the costumes to the door shedding the lights on the way. Cranleigh switched off the main light and followed Ann out. The door closed behind them.

A single ray of evening sunlight, percolating a small hole in the roof, fell upon the masked head of the executioner. A shadow left the dark behind the suit of armour and a grossly deformed hand reached into the light towards the triangular mask.

3

The Doctor Loses His Way

Standing by the huge fourposter bed that dominated the oak-panelled room the Doctor dangled the Pierrot costume from its neck, testing it for size. Lord Cranleigh looked on approvingly. The costume was of cream-coloured flannel extending in one piece from neck to feet. There was a deep scalloped collar and the arms, in slashed green and red check, ended in white mittens.

'It could have been made for me,' said the Doctor. He dropped the costume onto the bed and picked up the head covering which was all of a piece. The pale green cap that covered the head was fronted by a white face mask. This provided holes for the eyes and nostrils, and two blood-red triangles accentuated the cheeks. The Doctor put the head piece on and his identity promptly disappeared.

'I must flatter myself and call that an admirable choice,' said his Lordship. The Doctor's reply was muffled and so he removed the head piece and spoke again.

'It certainly is. What are you going to wear?'

'Nothing nearly as exotic. I shall do my best to impersonate Beau Brummell.'

'The eighteenth-century dandy?'

'Yes. The one who behaved abominably in Bath. But my impersonations will stop short at the clothes. There have been enough black sheep in the family without my adding to them.' He picked up the Roundhead costume from the foot of the bed. 'Now I must see to the young man. What was his name?'

'Adric.'

'Scandinavian?'

'Not quite. He's Alzarian.'

The Doctor felt quite safe in declaring Adric's origins. He knew the young nobleman would not offend good manners by pursuing the matter. Such lack of breeding was left to policemen, politicians and people from the press. Cranleigh was true to type.

'Never could remember all those funny Baltic bits,' he reflected. 'Geography was never my strong point. My brother stole all the thunder there. A positive Odin.' He moved to the door which he opened. 'Until later,' he said and withdrew.

The Doctor put the head piece with the rest of the Pierrot costume on the bed and took off his tail coat and v-necked sweater. As he did so he looked about him with satisfaction. His great age made him a natural antiquary and he warmed towards the solidity of Jacobean architecture and the mellow comfort of the furnishings. He went into the adjoining room to run his bath and saw, with amusement, the primitive unclad bath tub which was a concession to the early part of the twentieth century in traditional England. In high spirits after the vigorous and successful afternoon's sport he began to hum happily to himself.

'I think it could be a teeny-weeny bit tighter,' said Ann Talbot thoughtfully. She looked beyond the reflection of herself in the cheval-glass and at the figure of the maid-servant behind her who was adjusting the head-dress of her costume.

'Yes, miss,' agreed the maid. 'I'll just give it a tuck with a needle and thread.' She turned to riffle through the contents of a work basket on the table near the foot of the bed, leaving Ann to continue to primp and pat at the cleverly fashioned tulle dress that fell frothily from slender shoulder straps to a bunched hem just below her knees.

Both young women were too engrossed to hear a faint click at the wall beside the bed. The door in the panelling opened an inch or two in a sinister vertical black line; an elongated evil eye that watched unblinkingly as Ann's head-dress was fitted tighter.

*

Tegan hummed happily to herself, sinking deep into the armchair in another of the bedrooms in the guest wing.

'You sound happy,' said Nyssa, wrapping herself in the long housecoat that had been provided for her.

'I *am* happy,' agreed Tegan. 'A great game of cricket and a dance to look forward to. What more do you want?'

'You like it here, don't you?'

'Yes. Don't you?'

'No,' said Nyssa categorically. 'No, I don't.'

'Why not?'

'I don't know. There's something about the place ... a feeling. A feeling that I'm being watched.'

'Well, of course you're being watched,' exclaimed Tegan. 'It's only natural, isn't it? You and Ann looking like twins.'

'No, it's not that. It's more than that. Something creepy.'

'Creepy?'

'Yes.'

'It's the house,' said Tegan with authority. 'All old houses are the same and this one's bound to be haunted.'

'Haunted?'

'Ghosts,' explained Tegan cheerfully. 'Mary, Queen of Scots, I shouldn't be surprised ... with her head tucked underneath her arm.'

'Oh, don't!'

'Oh, come on, Nyssa! Cheer up! We're going to a dance ... a ball. You concentrate on that!' And Tegan began to whistle a jaunty, jerky tune which compelled her to rise and jig to it, knocking her knees together and kicking up her heels alternately.

'What *are* you doing?' asked Nyssa incredulously.

'It's called the Charleston.'

'That's dancing?'

Tegan stopped, aggrieved. 'It can't be that bad.'

'No, no!' said Nyssa hastily. 'I don't mean it's bad. On Traken our dancing is much more formalised. More of a ritual, really.'

'Show me!' demanded Tegan.

'Oh, I couldn't. Not by myself. You'd laugh.'

There was a tap on the door and Ann came in, followed by

her maid carrying two cardboard boxes. Ann was radiantly happy. 'My dears, I've had an absolutely *ripping* idea.'

For a moment Tegan was visited by a vision of the girl enthusiastically tearing clothes to shreds. Nyssa clapped her hands and stared with admiration at Ann's costume.

'Oh, how lovely! That's lovely!'

Pleased, Ann twirled this way and that, showing off the dress. 'I'm so glad you think so. But ... first ... Tegan.' She turned to the maid who took the lid from one of the boxes. 'This is for you,' and so saying she lifted up the taffeta dress. 'You're a wood nymph.' Tegan looked happily at the spritely confection of a dress. It suited her mood exactly.

'Thank you, Ann. That's nice. I shall enjoy being a wood nymph.'

Ann turned importantly to the other box. 'But just look what we've got here!' The maid removed the lid and Ann lifted from the box a costume identical to the one she was wearing. 'There! With the head-dress nobody, but nobody, will be able to tell us apart. Isn't that topping?'

Nyssa was thrilled. 'Quite topping,' she agreed. Tegan looked at the other two with quiet amusement. Identical dresses were anathema to female sartorial judgement except when it concerned twins it seemed.

Nyssa slipped into the dress excitedly. It fitted perfectly. With the head-dress in place and the long hair tucked underneath it the two girls were indistinguishable. Ann took Nyssa by the hand and turned to Tegan. 'See if you can tell us apart. Close your eyes, count to five and then open them again!'

Tegan did as she was bidden and Ann looked at Nyssa and put a warning finger to her lips. She then changed places with her twin. Tegan opened her eyes and looked at the two girls with pleasure and amusement.

'I'm only guessing but ... you're Ann,' she announced happily and pointed a finger.

'Wrong,' said Nyssa triumphantly and all three chuckled delightedly.

'This is going to be such fun,' said Ann.

'But not for poor Lord Cranleigh,' murmured Tegan.

'Oh, Charles will love it. He only has to do this.' Ann moved the left shoulder strap of her dress a little to one side to reveal a small mole. 'Unless you've got one too, Nyssa.'

Nyssa shook her head. 'Just as well,' said Tegan. 'It could lead to all sorts of complications if you put your mind to it.'

The Doctor had indulged himself with a good long soak in the bath reflecting that the afternoon's exercise, being exceptional, would remind him on the morrow of muscles he'd forgotten he had. It was the price the amateur cricketer paid for the opening game of the season and in the Doctor's case his extraterrestrial activity forbade seasonal involvement in a game demanding the teamwork of twenty-two English-speaking men or women. He towelled himself vigorously and hummed quietly to himself.

In the bedroom a barely audible click at the panelling beside the bed preceded the appearance of the vertical black slit that slowly widened until the gap was large enough to admit a figure wearing the executioner's triangular mask. The bed was between the secret door and the bathroom and the executioner crept slowly along the length of the bed to the foot of it as noiseless as a shadow.

The Doctor slipped into a dressing gown and vocalised the tune he was humming: *I want to be happy* ... The masked figure stopped near the foot of the bed and turned to look at the door in the panelling and then at the bedroom door which was closer. The executioner flitted to the door but had no time to open it before the Doctor came into the bedroom. The figure shrank into the deep shadow near the door. ... *but I can't be happy* ... *until I've made* ... The Doctor broke off as he saw the gaping hole in the wall by the bed. It was startling enough to absorb his whole attention and directed his eyes away from the shadow by the bedroom door as he made his way round the bed to the door in the panelling.

'Hello?' he said. 'Anyone there?' He advanced one foot into the void and again called, 'Hello?' He was answered by the hollow echo of his own voice. The Doctor withdrew his foot and examined the door closely. Such secret doors were a commonplace in houses of this period giving access, as they did, to priest holes – hiding places for the persecuted clergy and, at a later time, the Royalists hunted by the forces of Oliver Cromwell. The Doctor ran his fingers along the three edges of the door seeking a catch without success. There was always the possibility that the door may have opened of its own accord; a vibration perhaps? The Doctor's light baritone was hardly operatic but singers had been known to crack glasses with their voices; why not open doors? The Doctor shifted his attention from the door to the void beyond and, once again, his consuming curiosity was to prove his downfall. He stepped through the door, his eyes probing the dark.

The masked figure slid silently from the shadows and sped across the room. The door in the panelling snapped shut and the Doctor rounded in the dark to push against the door. 'Who's there?' He rapped on the panelling. 'Is anyone there? Hello?' Again his hands wandered about in vain exploration. On the other side of the secret door the executioner moved decisively to the foot of the bed. The deformed hands gathered up the Pierrot costume.

The Doctor abandoned his search for a door fastening in favour of deeper penetration into the dark. It was probable the area had another exit. He edged his way cautiously forward, testing the ground carefully one foot at a time while feeling the cold damp walls of the narrow passage with prying fingers. 'Why do I always let my curiosity get the better of me?' he muttered.

The thronged south terrace of the hall was pink and gold in the rays of the lowering sun. A band beat and howled the ragtime with the unabashed enjoyment peculiar to jazz musicians. Their happy sounds infected the multitude of dancers whose costumes ranged through history, literature and zoology with great diversity and originality. Lady Cranleigh's beautiful and elegant Marie Antionette was dancing with a striking Lewis Carroll Carpenter whose costume partner, the Walrus, was tripping the light fantastic with a rather large canary. Ann, dancing with her fiancé's Beau Brummell, exchanged a wink with her twin as Nyssa passed by on her way to join Adric who, excluded by shyness from the dancing, was casting appreciative eyes at the exotic cold buffet.

'When do we get to that?' he asked Nyssa quietly.

'Don't you think about anything else? And how did you know it was me?'

'I just know.'

'Oh!' Nyssa stamped her foot in irritation. Adric really was impossible at times. If Tegan couldn't tell which was which, how could he? But she wasn't going to let him spoil her evening. 'This is going to be much more fun than I thought,' she said. She looked across at Tegan who danced by with Sir Robert attired in flamboyant Restoration finery. 'I think you have to ask me to dance.'

'Why?' asked Adric vacantly.

Nyssa fought against the returning irritation. 'Because that's what everybody else has been doing.'

Adric's eyebrows arched high in disbelief. 'What! All these people?'

'Not me, you idiot! Each other. Come on! Ask me!'

Adric looked down at his feet and then at the feet nimbly moving all about him. 'I don't think I can do this,' he said disconsolately. 'Of course you can,' declared Nyssa bossily. 'Just follow me! Come on!'

Determined to enjoy herself to the full, Nyssa bore off the reluctant Adric. With a natural sense of timing she improvised brilliantly and was even able to communicate something of her expertise to her unwilling partner. Sir Robert watched them go by and smiled a little tightly to Tegan.

'I hope Lord Cranleigh has the right one. It's a little naughty really,' he chuckled.

'I think it's great hoot,' said Tegan briskly.

'A great what?'

'Hoot.'

'Hoot?' Sir Robert looked at his partner in some perplexity. Tegan smiled and pursed her lips in an audible pout that produced a sound rather like a laugh. The unusual word tumbled into place for Sir Robert. 'Ah, yes,' he said happily. 'Hoot.'

The Marquess of Cranleigh looked adoringly at the merry eyes laughing at him through the mask. They were unmistakably Ann's eyes for these were eyes that allowed him to see only that which was reserved for him. But he couldn't possibly tell her that, for it would spoil her fun and he did all he could these days to protect his future wife's new found happiness and contentment. She had come courageously through a sad time for them all.

'There is one way of not getting you mixed up,' he said. 'What's that?'

'To have every dance with you.'

'Foiled again,' she laughed. 'You're the host.'

The dance came to an end and both Nyssa and Ann waved to each other, a gesture which proved to be a pre-arranged signal. The girls ran to each other and flitted among the guests like a pair of dancing moths seeking the richest cloth onto which to home. As they moved they separated and rejoined from time to time, weaving in and out of sight in a choreographed shuffle of identities.

Lady Cranleigh frowned. A vague disquiet had taken a progressive hold on her since she had first seen the two girls dressed alike. It stirred a fear she had kept at a distance for so long. What was for everyone else a lighthearted prank was to her a reminder of a grave danger ... a danger that she could do nothing to lessen by sharing. As she watched the two girls flutter this way and that, she realised that she could no longer tell them apart. And if she could not ...

The clarinetist in the band had caught the mood of the moth dance and had begun to improvise a flighty tune to accompany it that owed not a little to something familiar by Mendelssohn. It delighted the guests and struck dread in the heart of Lady Cranleigh. She wanted to cry out and stop it but that was something she could never bring herself to do. Eventually the two moths joined for the last time, fluttered for a moment in the same spot and then dipped in a curtsey that signalled the end of their performance.

Enthusiastic applause was succeeded by a delighted buzz of speculation about which was which as the girls moved on Adric and Cranleigh. The band struck up again.

'Ann?' asked Cranleigh.

'Guess!' came the reply. Cranleigh smiled as he took the girl he knew to be Ann into his arms. 'Give me a little time,' he said.

'Well?' asked Nyssa.

'Very clever,' said Adric, meaning it.

'No. Which one?'

'Nyssa, of course.'

'Oh!' Nyssa pouted. 'That was just a guess.'

'No!'

'Oh!'

Poor Adric. It would only make matters worse if he attempted to explain to her that they'd been together long enough for him to be able to recognise certain of her little ways; her challenging stance, the set of her head when looking intently at anyone, the little intake of breath that preceded a sudden question. He was beginning to learn that in women there was no such concept as predictability. All the same he promised himself that if Nyssa tried it on him again he'd tell her.

'Where's the Doctor?' she asked.

'I don't know. He said he was going to have a bath.'

'That was hours ago.' Nyssa looked round at the whirling, kaleidoscopic dancers. The Doctor could be any number of anonymous personalities enjoying loss of identity in countless other characters. 'What's he wearing?'

'I don't know that either.'

Nyssa looked searchingly at Adric's costume. It was a look that was intended to be withering, to contain a comment on what Nyssa took to be wilful ignorance on Adric's part not to be more curious about what the Doctor was wearing. But the look also contained an element of envy as she admired the flounced flamboyance of a costume she knew would suit her admirably.

'What are you supposed to be?'

'A Cavalier or a Roundhead or something,' Adric

examined, for the umpteenth time, the unmanagable frills of lace round his cuffs that were always getting in the way and making him uncomfortably self-conscious.

'What are they?'

'I don't know.'

'Adric!'

'I didn't like to ask. It was worn by someone who used to live here. I didn't want to be rude.'

Adric was quite within his rights, of course, but it miffed Nyssa that this was something she had to admit to herself. And she wasn't going to let him get away with that.

'Well, if you don't want to be rude you'd better ask Lady Cranleigh to dance.'

Adric looked even more self-conscious and was grateful when someone who looked like a large egg interrupted them courteously and asked Nyssa to dance. The sight of Humpty Dumpty bearing Nyssa away reminded Adric of all those goodies arranged on the buffet tables.

The Doctor, still feeling his way slowly through the impenetrable mildewed dark, came to a dead end. He stopped suddenly as first a toe and then a hand made contact with a damp stone wall. He tried to still the apprehension that always preceded panic at the realisation that there was no apparent exit from his prison within the cavity of the walls. The very secrecy that protected the fugitive also threatened the unwitting intruder. But the Doctor knew that every entrance had to be balanced by an exit even if they might be coincidental. He began slowly to retrace his steps.

The erect military-looking gentleman masquerading as the Merry Monarch and dancing with Lady Cranleigh looked over his partner's shoulder with his mouth suddenly agape.

'By George, that's a good one!'

'What's that, colonel?'

'That feller's costume. And the make-up. Never seen anything like it.'

The colonel turned his partner in order for her to be able to take up his line of sight. Standing at the edge of the terrace watching the dancing was the South American Indian with the protuberant lower lip. Lady Cranleigh's pulse raced and she caught at her escaping breath.

'Damned ingenious,' went on the colonel enthusiastically. 'Who is it, d'you know?' Lady Cranleigh got control of herself quickly. In ordinary circumstances the Indian's appearance could only be conspicuous but at a fancy dress ball it was unexceptional save for the admiration it provoked at the guest's originality.

'Yes, I do,' said Lady Cranleigh quickly. 'If you'll excuse me, Colonel, I must go and greet him.'

'Of course, dear lady.'

Lady Cranleigh forced herself to keep her passage through the dancers slow enough not to arouse any curiosity in her guests, and approached the Indian sedately and with a welcoming smile which became tight-lipped once she had guided her unexpected guest to the shelter of an arbour at the end of the terrace.

'Dittar! What *are* you doing?' The Indian took his troubled eyes from the dancers and dropped them sorrowfully.

'There was nothing else for me to do.' He spoke precisely, deliberately, with very little accent.

'What's wrong?'

'My good friend has gone.'

'Gone? What do you mean, gone?'

The Indian's deep-set black eyes dwelt upon the tight lines of the woman's face with a profound sadness. 'When I arose today he was not in the room. Last night was the night of the moon.'

'Not in the room? What about Digby?'

'Digby, he also has gone.'

'Digby?'

'It was the night of the moon.'

'That's nonsense, Dittar, nonsense!' She spoke with uncontrollable anger born of a terrible fear. Reproach was added to the sadness in the black eye.

'Come with me!'

Lady Cranleigh hurried away through a dense rose garden to a distant green house followed closely by the Indian. Inside the green house, submerged in the proliferation of tropical foliage, the frightened woman turned to the Indian who gulped greedily at the sweet warm air.

'Now!'

'I would come to you sooner,' began the Indian apologetically, 'but it was not safe until the ceremony ... the ceremony of the dance of masks.'

Gratitude closely followed by a sense of shame helped Lady Cranleigh to hold her fear in check. She drew courage from the quiet strength of the dignified Indian whose primitive roots she knew to be deeper than her own.

'It was clever of you, Dittar. Thank you. But they must be somewhere.'

'I have searched through the day. There is no sign.'

She knew this to be true. If Dittar Latoni, Chief of the Utobi, could find no sign, there was no sign to find. And yet instinct told her there could be one place where the Indian had not searched. There were sacred areas in his own ancestor worship which bound him to respect that of others.

'Have you looked in the attic?'

'No, Lady.'

'Then come!'

4

The Doctor Makes A Find

The unrelieved blackness and the rank, damp air somehow made it difficult to breathe. The Doctor wanted nothing more than to suck light air into his labouring lungs; it took preference over the satisfaction of his inordinate curiosity. When adventuring from his room he had concentrated his attention on the wall to his right in the belief that a possible exit would be in the opposite wall. Now he was returning to the point where his inquisitiveness had held him firmly by the nose he again concentrated his manual exploration on the wall to his right to balance the possibility of finding an exit point even if it meant no more than a return to his room.

'Got it!' The expression of triumph leapt involuntarily from his lips as a hair-thin line of light slashed his hand at head height. He had missed the unmistakable join in the woodwork on his outward journey for the reason that his sight had had no time to adjust. But his eyes had long since surrendered to a bottomless blackness that, alone, made it possible for him to see the light. Such is the nature of humility, he thought. He would remember that.

All his fingers followed along the line of light probing for an irrelevance, an abnormality, something that contradicted the predictable. The little finger on his right hand found it; a thimble-sized knob that gave under pressure. A panel pivoted away from him with a groan and the Doctor stepped, gratefully, into a narrow corridor capped by skylights. Wherever he was he was directly under a roof.

The corridor was narrow, narrower than the corridor where his own room was situated, and there were doors to either side. The Doctor tapped on the first, turned the handle and pushed, expecting the door to open inwards. Assuming the door to be locked he stepped away from it but the pressure of his hand dragging on the handle pulled the door open revealing a cupboard. It was stacked with books. The Doctor picked one up and then another, glancing at their spines. They were both botanical works. Further examination told him that all volumes were on botanical or geographical subjects. The Doctor inferred that they represented the stored library of the late Marquess who had died in the Venezualan jungle. He moved on to the next door which, again, proved to be a cupboard. This one contained articles of men's clothing all neatly folded and stacked.

The remaining cupboards contained more books and clothing and one was filled with sporting equipment: cricket bats, tennis-rackets and croquet mallets. One door at the end of the passage was narrower than the rest. It proved to be empty but it was deeper than the others, the sort of cupboard used for keeping brooms and similar domestic articles. The Doctor stepped into it for a closer look and was startled by a squeak that suggested he had invaded the home of some small creature now perished underfoot. But the sound was no more than the back of the cupboard beginning to move; something that caused a relexive action in the Doctor. He lifted his foot and the back of the cupboard reversed its movement. The floor of the cupboard was clearly the spring which opened yet another secret door. The Doctor glanced back along the corridor to confirm that the panel through which he'd escaped was still open. With his retreat covered he felt more confident about continuing his exploration. He stepped into the cupboard and its back slid to one side to expose another passage way. This was, indeed, a house of secrets.

Dittar Latoni, Chief of the Utobi, hissed between his teeth. It was a noise rendered more plangent by the sounding board of the protruding lower lip. What came forth was a note from a Venezualan humming bird: a warning call used by hunters in the jungle on the banks of the Orinoco. Lady Cranleigh stopped and turned to look at the Indian. He signalled silently that he should precede her through the attic door. She shook her head. 'No, Dittar,' she said firmly. 'I have nothing to fear from your friend.'

'It is still the time of the moon,' replied the Indian gravely.

Lady Cranleigh stepped resolutely to the door and opened it. The Indian quickly closed the distance between them to protect her from any threat beyond as she felt for the switch and turned on the light. The room seemed empty except for the family memorabilia and the ghosts that undoubtedly haunted them.

'Are you here, friend of Dittar?' called Lady Cranleigh.

'Lady!' implored the Indian and moved protectively ahead of her, pushing his way further into the room. He eased between the baskets and the effigies, ducking and stooping to look behind them. He moved cautiously behind the suit of armour and straightened to look with sad eyes on the smooth, exposed, featureless face of the unmasked executioner.

'He was here, Lady.'

'How do you know?'

'I can smell him.'

Adric was feeling lonely, distinctly left out of it. He watched the cavorting dancers enviously, less envious of their prowess than their courage in making such fools of themselves. Nyssa had finally abandoned him and he was kicking his heels with a furtive eye on the resplendent buffet but he lacked the courage even to invade that single-handed. The last thing he wanted to be was conspicuous; more conspicuous than he felt in this ridiculous costume, that is. He'd suffered the last straw when a young man, dressed as what he discovered later was an eighteenth-century pirate, had approached him and asked him to dance. All he'd done was to open his mouth to say 'thank you' and the pirate had blushed, cleared his throat, muttered something about being sorry and beat a hasty retreat. It really was the limit.

He'd even thought of following Nyssa's suggestion and asking Lady Cranleigh to dance. He might make a perfect fool of himself but it would at least do something to reassert his masculinity. But Lady Cranleigh had disappeared from the scene. He cast longing eyes at the inviolate food. His mouth was uncomfortably dry. Perhaps he could ask one of those proud-looking frilly fellows for one of those lemon drinks.

The dancers were throbbing through a tango. Nyssa had watched her twin jerk through its unexpected rythms and then had readily accepted an invitation from a large white rabbit to join in. Sir Robert's full-bottomed wig whipped into the face of the twirling Tegan with the impetus of the dance in a way impossible for him to control.

'My dear, you deserve a better dancer than I. We must find you someone your own age.'

'You're a bute dancer, Sir Robert,' said Tegan pulling her head out of the path of the knight's flailing locks. Sir Robert considered her remark for a step or two before concluding it to be a compliment, and replied with a twinkling smile, 'That, surely, is a great hoot.'

Tegan chuckled. The dance came to an end and she looked across the terrace to where the twins had come together once more with their respective partners. Sir Robert followed her look. 'Miss Talbot and your friend are again impossible to tell apart. I wouldn't like to swear which is which.'

'There's a way of telling,' confided Tegan.

'What's that?'

'It's a secret.'

The band opened up again with a lively tune and Sir Robert looked rueful. 'I don't think I can manage this one.'

'The Charleston? Just watch me,' suggested Tegan. She shook and twitched her way into the dance watched by an admiring Sir Robert. 'Easy! See!'

Don Quixote claimed one twin, leading her away across the terrace with convulsive knee jerks that threatened to dislocate his armour. Adric moved to the other twin, confident about her identity. 'Enjoying yourself, Nyssa?'

Ann looked at the boy, her eyes sparkling from behind her mask. 'Nyssa? Can you be sure, Adric!' Adric grinned. He was quite sure. Nyssa was playing with him. She had altered her voice so that the delivery was softer and her eyes were wider in a more docile look. But she wasn't going to fool him. He

62

nodded after the twin with the galvanic man from La Mancha. 'You can't do that.'

'Can't I?' Ann swung into the dance effortlessly and Adric watched her nimble knees and kicking heels open-mouthed. He glanced away at the other twin to confirm that he wasn't seeing double. No, the dancing of both girls was as alike as their appearance. Adric shook his head, both crestfallen and amused. 'I give up,' he said.

'Don't do that! Come on! You try!' Ann shifted her weight from one leg to the other, her heels flying in time to the happy, catchy music.

Adric summoned all his courage. With a gulp and a giggle he had a desperate go at copying the pattern of his partner's busy feet. Ann clapped her hands in encouragement. 'That's it! That's the way!'

All at once a wave of happiness overcame Adric. He was doing it. Yes, he was doing it and felt wonderful!

The Doctor considered the three doors along the wall of this new passage. More cupboards? He approached the first one across floor boards unrelieved by the drugget that had softened his footfalls earlier. He met what lay beyond the door with mild surprise.

He looked at a small but very comfortable bed-sitting room. There was none of the imposing solemn grandeur of the important guest rooms he had seen. Here the furnishings were modern and cheerful. Underfoot was fitted green carpet of deep pile and good quality. There were books, flowers and a gramophone. The Doctor carefully picked up one of the brittle 78 rpm records and glanced at the title which was Spanish. No, not Spanish, he reflected, Portugese.

He returned to the passage and the next door in line. This room was similar. The same stark outline of the former but well-appointed, even luxurious. On a coathanger clipped over the open wardrobe door hung a short white coat. Clearly these rooms were currently occupied. What had once been hiding places for persecuted priests or hunted Royalists were in use again. Did they house modern fugitives?

The Doctor's troubled thoughts were further disturbed by the sound of distant voices. One, a woman's, was getting nearer. The Doctor, acting on instinct, tucked himself out of sight behind the open wardrobe door. He'd had no right to penetrate the secret passages of Cranleigh Hall but his protean curiosity demanded satisfaction about the nature of any fugitives seeking sanctuary here.

He had made his move only just in time. Someone had entered the room. He aligned an eye to the crack between the wardrobe edge and the door just below the upper hinge and saw a woman dressed as an eighteenth-century French aristocrat and another guest, parading as a South American rain forest Indian. He remembered Tegan's description of such a guest as they arrived at the Hall after the cricket match. Then the woman spoke again and the Doctor recognised his hostess, Lady Cranleigh.

'He can't just have disappeared,' she was saying. 'Where would he go?' The Indian shrugged and the Doctor realised that the man was no counterfeit but the rather disquieting real thing. 'I was convinced he was trustworthy,' continued Lady Cranleigh. 'Young, but to be trusted. Has he said anything to you?'

'No, Lady.'

'About not being happy here ... anything like that?'

'No, Lady.'

The Indian looked tired, ill. Lady Cranleigh looked round the room and then closed her eyes and put a hand to her head as if to assuage an ache. 'Could he have been bribed?'

'Bribed, Lady?'

'By your friend ... to take him away?' The Indian shook his head slowly and sadly. 'My friend had no money for a bribe.' Lady Cranleigh released a long sigh and turned to the door. The Indian stood aside and she went from the room.

Down the wide main staircase of the Hall came a figure costumed as Pierrot, the rôle assigned to the Doctor. Its progress was slow, even ponderous, but inexorable. A brooding power flowed from the unsighted vents in the opaque mask of painted pathos. Down, down the figure came, a danger, a deadliness in the deliberate descent. A figure of fun inviting pity, unreal, unfleshed but somehow ferocious.

A footman, carrying a laden tray across the hall beneath, paid the menacing figure little attention. To him it was but one more guest making his passage to the kitchens that much more urgent. The figure left the stairs and padded along the hall towards the music and the laughter on the terrace.

The Doctor had remained long enough in his hiding place to give Lady Cranleigh and the Indian time to move well away. He now crossed the room in quiet haste and opened the door to peer into the passage. All clear. No sound. He waited a moment longer before leaving the safety of the bedroom, closing the door quietly behind him. He moved on to the third and last door which stood a little ajar. He eased the door and found himself looking into a neat bathroom. At the end of the passage a flight of steps spiralled upwards. Cautiously, the Doctor began to climb.

On the terrace the Charleston had been succeeded by a waltz, the sedate movement of which was far better suited to the motley apparel of the gently swaying dancers. Adric, whose confidence had been so gloriously restored, ebbed and flowed ebulliently with *The Blue Danube* to the delight of his partner. So joyful was he at his new-found skill that the sight of a number of guests beginning to regale themselves at the buffet tables moved no interest in him. He was content to dance on rejoicing in the movement and the music and the rapport with the partner he was now sure could not be Nyssa.

Then he saw something that prickled the skin at the nape of his neck. Standing near the glass door at the edge of the terrace was the figure of a clown: a Pierrot, he was later to discover. But there was something about the figure that drove a wedge of fear into his happy mood. He couldn't think what it was about the figure that made him suddenly afraid. Was it something to do with the sightless black holes in the mask of the painted face? They seemed to be turned on him, only him, piercing him through and through. The figure held so still that, for a moment, Adric thought it could be nothing more than a lifeless effigy, a large party decoration. He looked away, but when he looked back again the figure was gone.

The Doctor neared the top of the steps to see that they stopped at a small landing with nothing beyond but a heavy wood door reinforced by iron brackets. It stood ajar. The Doctor considered the implications of this soberly. From the passage below there had been nowhere else to go but up these steps. Therefore, he had to assume that Lady Cranleigh and the Indian had come this way and were in the room beyond. If this was so, he had to face them, he decided. He had nothing to hide or be ashamed of. He had lost his way, that's all. He had seen a strange opening in the wall of his room which hadn't been there before and he'd investigated. Unfortunately, the panel had closed behind him and he couldn't get back. His only recourse was to go on and he'd found himself here. Sorry!

'Hello!' he called.

There was no answer. He waited in a chilling silence. 'Hello!' he called again. Still nothing. He continued to the landing and tapped on the door. A sixth sense distilled danger from the heavy atmosphere. Alert, he pushed at the door and it swung back, grunting on its solid hinges. Bracing himself the Doctor entered the room. It was empty.

The Doctor wasn't surprised to see yet another well-appointed room with ample evidence of being lived in. But unlike the rooms below the furnishing was opulent, with books and flower prints lining the walls. He looked at the tidy desk, the well-tended fireplace, the dining table, the deep armchairs and the luxurious bed before becoming aware of the distant dance music. He turned in the direction of the sound and saw the barred window. He moved round the room making a close examination of the walls. There had to be a secret exit to explain the disappearance of Lady Cranleigh and the Indian for, hiding in the bed-sitting-room below, he'd not heard the squeal of the cupboard door that had given him noisy access. And yet it was hardly likely that such a means of escape could exist so high up in what was obviously a tower. And then there were the barred window and the heavy door. This room was some sort of prison; a comfortable prison but, none the less, a prison. No, the walls would not yield. Then the Doctor reflected that if his hostess and her exotic companion hadn't climbed the steps to this place there must be another way out of the passage beneath.

Nyssa's expectation that this dancing would be fun hadn't been disappointed. She happily followed where the accomplished Lord Cranleigh led and was even happier to see that her twin had succeeded in drawing such a polished performance from young Adric. She smiled at her partner.

'I hope your financée doesn't think you're neglecting her,' she said.

The Marquess looked across the terrace to where Ann was taking an absorbed Adric through the complexities of the Foxtrot. 'I hardly dare disturb her,' he grinned. 'She's having such a ripping time. I hope you are,' he added gallantly.

'Absolutely ripping,' endorsed Nyssa.

'I'm glad.'

They glided among the dancers passing the Walrus and the White Rabbit, Tegan and the Carpenter, and the Pierrot standing stock-still in the centre of the moving throng.

'Ah, there you are, Doctor!' exclaimed his Lordship, 'I was wondering if you were all right. You look magnificent. I hope it's comfortable. Is it?'

The Pierrot said nothing, the sightless eyeholes directed at Nyssa. She suddenly shivered in the warm evening air when the Pierrot raised a hand as if in salutation. Cranleigh guided her away from the solitary figure.

'That's the Doctor?' asked Nyssa.

'Splendid, isn't he?'

The Foxtrot ended and Adric joined enthusiastically in the ripple of applause for the hard-working band. 'You're a wonderful dancer,' declared Ann, 'but I think I've monopolised you long enough. Let me introduce you to a friend of mine. She's a much better dancer than I am, and I think she deserves you.'

Adric glowed at the compliment, so much so that the sudden tap on the shoulder, that punctured his euphoria, more than startled him. He turned to look up into the painted Pierrot face and gasped. The empty eyes bored blackly into him and then moved nearer causing in Adric an involuntary step backward. But the Pierrot had merely bowed in courtly fashion and was now extending a shapeless, supplicatory hand towards Ann in a request for the next dance.

Ann, thinking she knew the identity of the masked man, accepted the invitation with a little curtsey and Adric watched her borne away by the Pierrot in a laborious quickstep. Adric's lip curled in quick contempt. Hadn't he proved himself a better dancer than this clownish usurper? He watched the uncertain progress of his late partner and turned towards the comfort of food and drink.

The Doctor left the foot of the steps from the tower and made his way along the passage, passing the bathroom and bedrooms and making for the panel at the back of the cupboard by which he'd come. He guessed the panel would be difficult to refind and was proved right when he gave it close examination. The surface of the partition wall was smooth and there were no tell-tale edges visible since the panel did not pivot but slid to one side. This must be the only exit and the one used by Lady Cranleigh and the Indian earlier, but it still bothered him a little that he'd not heard them use it.

First the Doctor put pressure along the whole length of the floorboard next to the wall, assuming that the mechanism that moved the panel would be triggered as for the other side. When this yielded nothing he felt along the entire length of the moulding that must border the opening. This also kept the closely guarded secret, so the Doctor began systematically to press every inch of the wall within the moulding. This diligence was rewarded when his left hand reached a mark half way down the inside of the vertical carving. A small area gave under the pressure from his fingers and the panel slid away to the left with a low, practiced sigh. The Doctor stepped through onto the squealing floorboard and opened the cupboard door into the other corridor, the panel returning to the closed position behind him.

Then he saw, with shock, that the door from the wall cavity that he'd left open was now closed. He moved past the cupboards to the place in the wall that held the pivotting panel, cursing himself for not thinking of wedging it open in some way on his outward journey. He hadn't, of course, anticipated that the sortie from his room would result in a dead end. Here even his systematic manual search was of no use. The spring for this panel could be anywhere along the whole wall. A daunting prospect.

'I know you're the Doctor,' insisted Ann, 'because that was the costume picked out for you.' The Pierrot shook his head slowly and firmly several times. 'Then if you're not the Doctor who are you?' The Pierrot said nothing, dancing on, the sightless black eyes never moving from Ann's face. Ann laughed nervously. 'It's really rather creepy. Please tell me who you are.'

She and her silent partner had danced to within speaking distance of her fiancée a couple of times, and on these occasions Cranleigh had beamed upon her and nodded with easy familiarity at the disregarding Pierrot which had suggested to Ann that her partner was indeed the Doctor.

The dance came to an end with the drummer beating out the characteristic roll that announced the band was about to take a short break but the Pierrot danced on, taking Ann with him across the terrace towards the windows of the drawing room.

'The music's stopped,' said Ann, but if her partner heard her he paid no attention. She tried to remove her hand from his but her action only caused the grip about it to tighten. 'Please!' gasped Ann. 'You're hurting me! *Please!*' But she was whirled on towards the windows.

She looked back at the other dancers but those who were not drifting towards the buffet tables were looking at her with amusement. The mask she wore effectively hid her unhappy expression from the watching Nyssa.

'What *is* the Doctor doing?' Nyssa wanted to know.

'I fancy it's more a case of what Ann's doing,' suggested Lord Cranleigh. 'My guess is that she's up to some prank involving you both. We'll know soon enough. Come, let me get you some refreshment.' He gently but firmly steered her away.

Working his way methodically along the wall, the Doctor had come close enough to the other end of the corridor to see something that had escaped his notice: another door. It had no jamb or surround like the others, being flush to the wall and was thus invisible to the Doctor when he first came out of the dark behind the wall of his room. The only indication that it was a door came from the small catch that served as a handle. The Doctor grasped it and pulled.

What lay beyond was no way back to the rest of the house but another cupboard. It contained no books ... no clothes. Just several cardboard boxes and the crumpled body of a young man dressed in a short white coat, whose eyes were wide open and fixed in death.

5

The Pierrot Unmasked

Ann's unhappy bewilderment had smouldered into anger.
This really was beyond a joke. She guessed her mysterious
partner must be one of the visiting cricket team; a young man,
outside her set, taking liberties because he'd already had too
much to drink.

'Stop this!' she commanded. 'Stop it, I say!' But the bizarre
gyration continued in the centre of the drawing room. Ann
tried again to pull away from the implacable grip on her left
hand but succeeded only in painfully wrenching her
shoulder. 'You're hurting me!' she cried.

For answer the Pierrot pulled her to him and seized her
other hand. Gasping protests, Ann was pirouetted through
the doors and into the hall to the foot of the stairs where the
manic movement stopped. Again Ann tried to pull free but
the grip on her was unrelenting.

'All right!' she gasped furiously. 'You've had your fun.
Now stop it, d'you hear!'

She glared at the painted mask the bottom part of which
was given an incongruous movement by the rasping
breathing beyond; a sucking in and exhalation of breath that
was accompanied by a sinister, guttural clicking.

Ann's fury turned abruptly to fear. Suddenly she knew this
was no joke. Suddenly she knew she was in great danger. The
advance of cold terror had a curious calming affect on her: the
cool consideration of a dangerous situation that is the birth of
courage.

'If you don't let me go,' she said quietly, 'I shall call for
help, whoever you are.'

The clicking beyond the mask changed to a low groan

followed by a gurgling, inarticulate answer to her appeal. Ann found herself being drawn by powerful arms even nearer to the fearful Pierrot. She screamed. 'Help!'

The Pierrot pulled her towards the stairs with Ann wrenching at the grip of her attacker's hands and kicking at his legs. Time and time again the toes of her shoes made desperate, brutal contact of which her persecutor seemed oblivious. Her screams intensified. 'Help, somebody! *Help!*'

A footman came from the drawing room carrying an ice bucket in which were several empty champagne bottles. He had heard the cries for help before seeing the couple struggling together at the foot of the stairs. He hesitated. He was a servant and was in no position to question the behaviour of guests even if that behaviour was violent. It was above his station in life to comment publicly on the horseplay of his superiors. Such high jinks had to be ignored. The gentry had laws unto themselves and the privacy of their own homes included the total discretion of their servants. The footman continued imperturbably on his way.

'James!'

The scream stopped the footman in his tracks. He turned and saw anguish on Ann's face in spite of the half mask, and he had been directly named. 'Help me! Help me, please!' The Pierrot was growling now like a ravening animal and a ferocious effort had dragged Ann to the third tread of the stairs.

'Help me, James! *Help me!*'

The footman made up his mind that this was no upper class game. His employer's fiancée needed assistance whatever consequence intervention by a servant might have. He put down the ice bucket and ran to the stairs. The Pierrot pushed Ann from him and turned on the footman with a guttural cry. The servant's move had effectively rescued Ann and the man was inhibited by an innate servility from going further and laying hands on the sacred person of a guest in the house.

The hesitation gave the Pierrot an advantage. He pounced upon the footman and whirled him about to lock an arm round the unfortunate man's neck. Ann looked on in horror as the servant's mouth gaped and his eyes bulged. She rushed at the Pierrot, striking at the hidden face with tight fists but was held back by the unoccupied arm. She heard a bright snap and watched the footman collapse from the knees and roll from the stairs to the floor. Ann opened her mouth but what was born as a scream died as a sigh, as shock robbed her of consciousness. She dropped in a heap on the stair treads. The Pierrot stooped to her, advancing massive covered hands.

The Doctor felt inside the dead man's jacket and found an inner pocket from which he took a small leather wallet and an opened envelope that obviously contained a letter. The envelope was addressed to Mr Raymond Digby, Poste Restante, Bicester, but the wallet held no corroboration of identity, merely a ten shilling note and three postage stamps.

The Doctor withdrew the letter from the envelope. Its contents were short. It was from an address in London, began *Dear Son* and was signed *your affectionate Mum*. She told him how much she had enjoyed his visit last Sunday and hoped he was well, not working too hard, and continued to be happy in his new job – whatever it was – though she hoped and prayed he was doing nothing wrong, nothing bad. The Doctor replaced the wallet and letter, rose to his feet and closed the cupboard door. Judging by the degree of rigor mortis the man had been dead at least twelve hours. Once again fate had directed the Doctor's steps towards mysterious violence and deadly danger; but fate couldn't be relied upon to direct his steps from this secret labyrinth.

The Doctor moved quickly to the cupboard at the other end of the corridor. The room in which he'd hidden from Lady Cranleigh and the Indian had clearly been the dead man's temporary home; the white coat that hung there was similar to the one on the dead man. The two bedrooms, the bathroom and the room in the tower were a secret suite but there had to be some access to the main house. He would start in the dead man's room and seek a clue there. He opened the door and entered the cupboard to the predictable squeal. The panel in front of him hissed to one side and he stepped through into the other corridor.

'Doctor!'

Lady Cranleigh and the Indian stood half way down the corridor outside the dead man's door. The Indian stepped forward.

'It's all right, Dittar, the Doctor is a guest.'

The Indian stopped but his deep, black eyes remained fixed on the Doctor as if sensing danger. Lady Cranleigh drew level with him, her beautiful face coping with a tense smile.

'Doctor, this is Dittar Latoni, a friend from Venezula.'

'How do you do?' the Doctor nodded.

'Sir,' responded Latoni with a watchful respect.

Somehow the Doctor knew he wouldn't be asked to explain his presence in this secret part of the house. It wasn't just that questions were bad form; Lady Cranleigh had about her an air of controlled calm as if intent on accepting this intrusion as a perfectly normal course of events.

'I'm afraid I got lost,' admitted the Doctor.

'Yes,' Lady Cranleigh returned evenly.

'There was a door . . . a secret panel . . . open in my room. I went through it thinking there was someone there, and it closed behind me. I couldn't open it again so I felt about a bit in the dark and came out in a corridor through there . . . but I couldn't find a way out of that either . . . except through to here.'

'I'm sorry, Doctor. Six bedrooms and two of the reception rooms have access to this area.'

'A larger than average priest hole.'

'The Cranleighs of the time were devout. The priesthood came here from all over the country. And then, after that, the Royalists. King Charles and Prince Rupert both stayed here.'

'Really?' The Doctor sensed that the information was prompted less by family pride than by the need to preserve a passivity which Lady Cranleigh didn't feel. He also sensed that if he confessed to his earlier explorations he would cause acute embarrassment, but there was this dead body. 'And still in use,' he went on probingly.

'Oh, yes,' admitted Lady Cranleigh freely, 'the servants are here now.' The Doctor had no choice but to admit what he'd seen and there was very little he could do to cushion the awfulness of his discovery. He spoke as gently as he could.

'I'm very much afraid that in trying to find the way back to my room I found something very shocking.' He was watching Lady Cranleigh carefully and saw how little the proud mask slipped; the merest tremor on the mouth, the barely perceptible change of light in the eyes.

'Oh, Doctor?'

'Have you a servant called Digby?'

'Yes,' replied Lady Cranleigh, in a voice little above a whisper.

'I'm afraid he's dead – and I think he was murdered. He's been put in a cupboard in the next corridor.' The Doctor pointed in the direction of the panel that had closed behind him and watched the two exchange a look. He marvelled at the chiselled calm of the woman's face but was deeply disturbed that neither she nor the Indian seemed surprised by his statement.

He stood aside to let Lady Cranleigh approach the panel. Her hand found the activating spring without hesitation and the back of the cupboard slid to one side. Lady Cranleigh stepped into the squealing gap and the Doctor allowed the Indian to go next. As he followed them into the corridor he decided to explore further the lack of surprise at the servant's sudden death. He had it in mind to wait and see if either might already know where the body was hidden. He was answered when Lady Cranleigh turned and looked back at him enquiringly.

'The one at the end . . . facing us.'

Lady Cranleigh accepted the information unflinchingly and walked with determination to the cupboard at the end of the corridor. 'Lady!' said the Indian urgently as she reached it, but she wasn't to be deflected from tugging open the door.

Lady Cranleigh looked down at the twisted body of the young man just long enough to effect recognition and then turned away. She made a small gesture with the right hand which the Indian interpreted as a request to close the cupboard door.

The Doctor studied the noble face intently. The eyes were

far away in a remote sorrow. There was no mistaking the total lack of surprise at the death or at the discovery of it, but there was also no mistaking the deep compassion she felt. 'Poor fellow,' she whispered. 'The poor fellow.'

The Doctor shifted his gaze to the Indian. This South American native, with the grotesque lower lip, couldn't be more out of place in this stately English home but it was plain he lived here; the Portugese gramophone record in the other secret bedroom pointed to that. Portugese was a rarity in a country whose language was assumed to be the *lingua franca* of half the world but to the natives of large areas of the South American continent Portugese was a second language, a centuries old legacy from its colonists. What was the man doing here? In ordinary circumstances the Doctor would have little trouble in finding out but here, in this house and at this time, he was denied the direct question; good manners inhibited his insatiable curiosity as firmly as steel chains.

'Doctor?' His train of thought was brought to an abrupt halt by Lady Cranleigh. He turned to look at her and found himself under a strange scrutiny from the formerly sorrowful eyes which now held only suspicion. 'How did you know his name?'

The Doctor was suddenly unsettled by what looked remarkably like an accusation. Surely he wasn't suspected of having some hand in this deed? He needed time to think.

'I beg your pardon?'

'You said that Digby was dead when you found him?'

'Yes.'

'Did you know him?'

'Know him?'

'From before, I mean.'

'No.'

'Then how did you know his name?'

'There's a letter in an inside pocket.'

'A letter?'

'Yes. I assumed it was addressed to him.' The Doctor had become aware of a sudden change in the woman's controlled demeanour. The eyes glittered with a new alertness. 'Did you read the letter?'

The Doctor hesitated. It was true that his curiosity had got the better of him but why should she think he might have read the letter? And, even more important, why was she surrendering to a vulgar curiosity that was quite out of character for her, if not for him? Even as he hesitated he saw her alertness turn to something akin to panic. He decided on an answer that told the whole truth so far as he knew it.

'Yes. I did.'

'Why?'

'I'm not sure. I suppose it was to confirm the letter was his.'

'And was it?'

The Doctor considered the tight muscles in her face. This woman was very frightened. 'I think so.'

'You think so?'

The Doctor knew there was no question in Lady Cranleigh's mind about the identity of the dead man. She had admitted to knowledge of Digby and she had seen the body. Clearly the name and the corpse were not contradictory. What Lady Cranleigh wanted to know was the content of that letter. 'Why don't you look for yourself?' he asked. The woman's fear gave way to disdain. She turned away as if, suddenly, the Doctor was beneath contempt.

'How could you possibly suggest such a thing?' she said. 'It would be most improper. Such things must be left to the police.'

The Doctor was rebuked but he had it in his heart to help his troubled woman. His instinct told him that she knew more than she was prepared to admit but also that she must be innocent of any complicity in murder. He found himself saying, 'There's nothing in the letter that would help the police.'

'Help them?'

'To explain why he died. It's a letter from his mother. Quite short. Saying how nice it was to see him again. That's all.' He forebore to say that the mother was curious about the nature of her son's job and was anxious lest it be something unlawful. He forebore to say that the whole tone of the letter implied that Digby's employment was a close secret. He saw some of the anxiety drain from Lady Cranleigh's face but left behind were suspicious shadows and haunted eyes. He had seldom felt more uncomfortable. The haunted eyes searched his.

'I'm deeply sorry, Doctor, that you've had this dreadful experience.'

'No less dreadful for you, Lady Cranleigh.'

'But you are a *guest* in this house.' Lady Cranleigh couldn't be more regal than the queen she was dressed to resemble had been when she suggested that the breadless of Paris eat cake. 'I would be most grateful if you would help me keep this unpleasantness from my other guests. I wouldn't want to upset them.'

In the circumstances the request was reasonable enough but the Doctor couldn't drag himself away from the thought that he was being suborned to keep secret the discovery of the crime, and that was not to be tolerated. A certain relaxation of strain had not extended to Lady Cranleigh's alertness. She read the Doctor's thoughts.

'It's pointless involving them until the police decide otherwise,' she explained.

Lady Cranleigh's inclusion of the law in seeking to protect her guests from unpleasantness mollified the Doctor. 'You can rely on my discretion, Lady Cranleigh,' he said.

'You're very kind, Doctor.'

The Doctor looked down at his borrowed dressing gown. He suddenly felt vulnerable in his deshabillé next to the exotic Indian and the elegant French queen and he was anxious to spare his hostess any further embarrassment. 'If I may ask someone to point me in the direction of my room . . .'

Lady Cranleigh's whole tone and manner briskened. 'Of course. We're just behind it.' Her turn to the panelled wall was stopped by a sudden thought. 'And, Doctor, I'd be most grateful if you would . . . how shall I say . . . keep up appearances.'

'You mean . . . carry on in costume.'

'Exactly.'

'Of course. I'm quite taken by the idea.'

'Thank you.'

Lady Cranleigh turned again to the panelling and put out

78

and. At first the Doctor thought the slight noise from behind the woodwork was made by the mechanism that opened the panel but he then saw that lady Cranleigh's hand had stopped short of the wall as she, too, had heard the noise. The Doctor was conscious of a slight movement from the Indian and when he turned to the man found himself being looked at with watchful passivity. There was someone ... something ... behind that wall, in that sullen black cavity the Doctor had tried so hard to escape from.

The face Lady Cranleigh turned on the Doctor was calm and once more under her firm control. Even her tone was light. 'But no. I can't ask you to endure that again. And it's difficult to find the switch to your room panel. There's a more comfortable way. If you'll follow me, Doctor.' She moved regally to the far end of the corridor and again dipped her towering white wig into the confines of the cupboard linking the corridors. Once through she turned and said something in Portugese. She spoke so quietly and rapidly that the Doctor, whose knowledge of the language was hardly profound, failed to understand what was plainly an order. The Indian said nothing but retreated into the cupboard and the panel closed behind him.

The Doctor followed Lady Cranleigh to the foot of the steps that led to the room in the tower. She stopped by the newel and the Doctor learned why his thorough search of the walls for a way out of the secret area had gone unrewarded. Lady Cranleigh tugged at a carved acorn on the post and a panel in the wall opposite growled quietly open.

'Ah!' ejaculated the Doctor. Lady Cranleigh led the way through to the main corridor on the second floor of the Hall proper. She touched another piece of carving and the panel repeated its low growl as it closed behind them. The Doctor felt relief at the sight of familiar surroundings and smiled. It was answered by Lady Cranleigh.

'Your room is the first on the right, Doctor. And thank you again.'

The Doctor knew this to be a polite reminder of his promise not to embarrass her guests. He bowed his head in acknowledgement and watched his hostess move to the stairs and descend.

On the terrace the caparisoned guests clustered or ebbed and
flowed in pursuit of friends or acquaintances with Lord
Cranleigh dutifully playing host in the absence of his mother.
All nibbled at food or sipped delicately from slim glasses. All,
that is, with the exception of Adric who was doing justice to
the excellent fare with gusto, uninhibited by the convention
never to demonstrate a healthy appetite and always to
abandon a quantity of food on the plate.

Nyssa was talking to a burly young Roman centurion,
although it would be truer to say that the centurion was
talking to her since what was being said was in the nature of a
monologue about how he stroked, as she understood it, eight
men in a boat on a river called the Thames. He had, by all
accounts, stroked them to victory last year. She pondered
deeply how such an activity could be victorious and was
sorely puzzled about the day's preoccupation with birds,
ducks on the cricket field, cocktails in the bath and, now,
another winged creature, blade on the feather. She was
grateful for the interruption by Lord Cranleigh.

'Ann?' She turned to him.

'The other one.'

'Nyssa.'

'Yes.'

'It's nothing short of uncanny,' said Cranleigh in
delighted wonderment, 'how closely you resemble each
other.' He looked at the centurion. 'Don't you think so,
Tiny?'

'Uncanny,' agreed the stroker enthusiastically.

'Where is Traken exactly?' asked his Lordship gently.

Nyssa looked about her in a mild panic. She had been
rescued from the stroker but who would rescue her from the
charming Lord Cranleigh? Ann perhaps? But where was
Ann? She voiced the thought as the next best avenue of
escape.

'You were looking for Ann? I haven't seen her for some
time. The last time I saw her she was with the Doctor.' She

could tell from the opaque expression on Cranleigh's face that she hadn't succeeded in diverting interest from her origins and added, 'He's not been about for some time, either.' His Lordship smiled engagingly as if he knew she was temporising and she was desperately thinking about what she could say next when help came from an unexpected quarter.

The couple impersonating the Walrus and the Carpenter passed by on their way to join a group, which included the Queen and Knave of Hearts, acknowledging Lord Cranleigh as they did so. They had danced incongruously with other partners almost from the time of their arrival but now, together, they made a sort of literary sense that was even more incongruous to any unaware of their identity. Nyssa grasped at the passing straw.

'What are they?'

'The Walrus and the Carpenter.'

'The what?'

'The characters in *Through the Looking-glass*.'

'Oh?' said Nyssa, inflecting the sound as interestingly as she could in the expectation of more information. She wasn't disappointed.

'*Alice*. You must know the book.'

'No.'

'Oh!' responded his amazed Lordship involuntarily. He recovered and continued. 'Well, the Walrus and the Carpenter conspired against some oysters.'

'Oysters?'

'Oysters,' repeated the bemused nobleman.

'Why?'

'They wanted something to eat.'

'The oysters?'

'Yes ... no, the Walrus and the Carpenter wanted something to eat.'

Nyssa looked with delight at her host's earnest face. She had, indeed, succeeded in changing the subject. 'What's an oyster?' It was Lord Cranleigh's turn to look desperate. Wherever Traken was it must be remote; very out of touch. 'It's a shellfish.' He glanced towards the buffet tables. 'If there was an "r" in the month I could show you.' And then he saw a way out of the conversational impasse. 'Let me help you to a little collation.' He offered his arm to Nyssa and steered her towards the ever-ready social nostrum of food and drink.

The Doctor closed the door of his room behind him, his eyes going involuntarily to the panel by the bed, half expecting it to be open. The Pierrot costume had been returned; replaced in exactly the same spot from which it had been taken. But since the Doctor was unaware of its temporary and sinister absence it held no interest for him. He went to the panel and his fingers methodically sought a means of opening it without success. He was about to persist and repeat the examination when he remembered Lady Cranleigh's last demonstration. The mechanism could be anywhere in the room. He shrugged and turned his attention to the costume on the bed.

Tegan sipped at her champagne and looked around the terrace, watched by Sir Robert Muir. 'An interesting turn out,' he suggested.

'Yes. I was wondering where the Doctor was.'

'Not being bored by the old codger, I hope?'

The remark startled Tegan almost to the point of shock since it had been made by someone whom she considered neither old nor boring. Impulsively she touched the elegant knight's arm lightly and reassuringly. 'Oh, Sir Robert, of course not.'

His eyes ranged among the chattering and laughing groups on the terrace. 'There are any number of well covered up chaps of the right size and shape. The Doctor could be any one of them since he wants to remain incognito. My guess is that it's the man's innate modesty.'

Tegan smiled to herself. The Doctor? Innately modest?

'Have you known him long?' asked Sir Robert.

'The Doctor?'

'Yes.'

'A fair while.' Her tone was such that it discouraged further questions on the subject; a hint taken readily by the courtly

Sir Robert. He held out a hand. 'Let me help you to a thimbleful more of this excellent champagne.'

Ann Talbot lay insensible on the bed in the tower room. A sudden, sharp intake of breath began her revival. Her eyelids fluttered and then opened. Slowly her eyes focussed on the bars at the window, touched with gold by the evening sun. She looked at the window uncomprehendingly for a moment before turning her eyes on the flower prints and books lining the wall with equal incomprehension. Where was she? The question filled her mind, blocking all memory of the moment before she lost consciousness. She turned her head and a sudden muscular contraction, provoked by extreme terror, robbed her of breath. Her mouth opened in an agonising, noiseless scream.

A creature stood by the bed looking down at her. It was in some sort of human shape but was so monstrously deformed as to deny all evidence of humanity. The trunk and legs were dressed conventionally in an open-necked shirt, a pullover in large diamond check, and grey flannel trousers. The head, face, forearms and hands were such that they could have been fashioned in wax and then melted beyond recognition in a fire.

The head was hairless with exposed and alternative livid and puce puckered skin. Human facial features were barely acknowledged. There were no recognisable ears. The eyes were hideously shot with blood, the right one almost submerged in folds of livid morbid flesh. A fleshless ridge with two perforations and a lipless gash beneath it was small evidence of a nose and mouth. The obscenely puckered forearms supported hands, the fingers of which were welded together, giving a grotesque prominence to the thumbs.

The gash widened and a clicking came from the back of the throat.

Ann pushed at the bed with her hands struggling to get up, her lungs fighting painfully for breath, her eyes forced wide in uncontrollable terror. She sucked in enough air to voice a horrible, rattling scream.

The creature's visible eye closed for a moment and its hands came up in front of its monstrous face. Ann screamed again and scrambled free from the bed, her eyes on the distant, iron-clad door. The creature lowered its hands and moved to block her path, the clicking from the throat becoming louder and faster. Extending its hands, the creature began slowly to move on Ann. She backed away and tried again to scream but no sound would come. She fetched up against the wall and pushed out the palms of her hands to hold off the moving monster. The creature stopped and sank to its knees, its arms outstretched. Ann's scream was loosed at last. The creature lifted the fused fingers of one hand and put them at a right angle to the gash in its face. Ann's eyes turned upwards under her lids. She sighed and slid to the floor.

The creature began to crawl towards her.

6

The Pierrot Reappears

The Doctor looked at his reflection in the cheval-glass with some satisfaction. He donned the head piece and smiled behind the painted mask at the reflected stranger before him. He bowed ironically to discover that his own tail coat, beneath the fancy dress, inhibited free movement. He'd be better off without it. He removed the head piece and began to undo his costume.

It was only natural, he supposed, that Lady Cranleigh should wish the ball to be continued without embarrassment or alarm. The elaborate façade, erected by what was known as high society in this period, hid many social skeletons in many murky cupboards. As many ills and as much unpleasantness as possible were masked from those of delicate sensibility by a cult of good manners in which hypocrisy played a very grubby part. Victorian and Edwardian values in England had survived the revealing Great War in Europe and the still powerful upper and middle classes set great store by the preservation of a social fabric which was now under threat from the vulgar, the self-seeking and the envious.

The body he'd discovered was corporeal enough but it flitted into the good Doctor's mind that it was not unknown for distinguished piles to house dry, clandestine bones and the dead Digby could be, at one time, well qualified for such a fate. Why not now? No, the police were to be called. The Doctor dismissed the thought. Nevertheless Cranleigh Hall did contain some closely guarded secret and had been penetrated by a killer. Could they be one and the same?

*

Ann again lay on the bed, her eyes closed and her face shiny with sweat, but unharmed. The creature sat on the bed, the bloodshot eye fixed on the girl who was twitching with the unconscious reflex actions of a suppressed terror. The creature slowly put out a hand and gently touched the tortured, pretty face. A muscle shivered beneath the touch and the creature snatched back the hand as if it had been hurt. The inflamed eye closed and the hand was put to the gash in the face in an acknowledgement of pain.

A sound from the other side of the door turned the creature's repulsive head, the eye wide with alarm. Slowly, the savage deformity rose from the bed to face the door squarely, the melted hands lifting defensively.

In spite of herself Lady Cranleigh flinched from the other side of the door and signalled to the Indian to take her place. He did so and grasped the handle to turn it. The door was unyielding.

'It is locked, Lady' the Indian whispered. Lady Cranleigh closed her eyes, her face compressed in pain. The Indian knocked on the door with his knuckles.

'My friend, it is I. Open!'

The creature did not move. The Indian spoke again. 'My friend! My good friend, open for me!' The creature's burning eye looked at the key in the lock but still it did not move.

The Indian knocked again and waited. Then he turned to look at Lady Cranleigh shaking his head. Taking a determined grip on her wide, flowing skirt Lady Cranleigh moved to the head of the steps and hurried down out of sight. The Indian knocked again.

'My friend! My good friend, do not part us in this way! You will come to harm. You will be unhappy. Open, please!'

The creature hadn't moved but the knocking and the raised voice broke into Ann's consciousness and she stirred. Immediately the creature rounded on her, the gap in the face panting open, the clicking in the throat responding to the increased pattern in breathing. The Indian continued to rap on the door with repeated entreaties for his friend to let him in.

Ann opened her eyes and instantly recalled where she was.

A cry escaped her dry throat and she swallowed, gulped in air, and rolled from the bed. The Indian heard her with dread in his heart. What he'd prevented so often before had finally taken place. He prayed to his gods no harm would come to the Lady Talbot and renewed his knocking.

'My friend!'

'Help me!' Ann screamed. 'Help me!'

The creature held out his arms to her and again fell to his knees. The Indian threw his weight against the door impotently, knowing it had been made to withstand much more than all the strength he could muster. Ann screamed again and the Indian called: 'Lady! Lady, help is here.' His voice startled Ann into a sort of steadiness but she began to weep chokingly.

The Indian bounded down the steps on the way to his room in search of something with which he could realistically attack the door. The terrified Ann looked at the kneeling creature, her small frame racked with sobs. The gash in the creature's face opened wide and the rapid clicking increased horribly.

Then Ann saw the tear drip from the creature's eye and dribble down the hideous puckered skin. Instantly she sensed that she was in no danger and her sobbing subsided, but it was some time before she could trust herself to speak.

'Who are you?'

The clicking appeared to take on a pattern.

'What are you?'

Another tear followed the first. Clearly the creature was trying to speak. Ann brushed aside her own tears. She looked intently at the gaping gash whence came the clicking. The creature had no tongue.

Ann began to weep again but this time the tears were not provoked by terror but by compassion.

The Indian rushed empty-handed from his room as Lady Cranleigh came through the panel opposite the foot of the steps holding a large key. She held it up to the Indian who took it, saying urgently, 'He has the Lady Talbot.'

Lady Cranleigh's eyes went wide with shock as the Indian raced up the steps. She hurried after him as fast as her wide skirt would allow her. 'Lady!' called the Indian through the door. No sound came from the other side and the Indian avoided looking at Lady Cranleigh as she left the steps for his side.

'Ann!' she cried. 'Ann!'

Silence.

The Indian attempted to put the key in the lock with an anxious, unsteady hand before realising that the keyhole was blocked by the key inserted from the inside. He looked fearfully at Lady Cranleigh. 'The key is on the inside,' he whispered.

'Push it through, man!' said Lady Cranleigh fiercely. 'Push it through!'

The Indian again attacked the lock with the spare key but the one in the lock resisted all pressure.

Ann was too affected by the sorrowing creature to respond to Lady Cranleigh's cries from beyond the heavy door and, for the same reason, was oblivious of the metallic tapping and scratching as the Indian probed the lock. She felt drawn to the monstrous deformity kneeling pathetically before her. She eased slowly forward. 'Don't cry!' she said softly through her tears. 'Don't cry!'

'Ann!' called Lady Cranleigh desperately. 'Ann!'

The creature's burning eye brimmed and his webbed hand snatched at Ann's fingers. Ann blenched and shivered as revulsion returned to her. She felt her fingers being pulled nearer to the gashed face and, with a frightened gasp, wrenched her hand free. She ran to the door, turned the key and tugged at the handle. The door was pushed open by the Indian and Ann ran out to the landing and into the open arms of Lady Cranleigh.

The creature had not moved. Handing the spare key back to Lady Cranleigh, the Indian slipped into the tower room and closed the door quietly on the two women. Held in comforting arms Ann wept anew, unable to speak.

'There, there,' murmured Lady Cranleigh, 'There, there.'

The Indian relocked the door from the inside and pocketed the key. He moved to the creature which had sat back on its haunches and was rocking to and fro and moaning softly.

'Oh, my friend.' The Indian helped the creature to its feet and steered it with infinite gentleness to the bed where he encouraged it to sit. He sat beside it and took a hideous hand in both of his. 'Oh, my friend, forgive me! It is the time of the moon, of the ripe moon, and I should not have left you. I should not have left you to the other one. But I am here with you again. You shall rest and all will be well again. Contentment will come to you.'

Rising from the bed the Indian approached a white-painted metal cabinet fixed to the wall between bookshelves. He selected one of the small keys that hung in a bunch from a chain about his neck and opened the cabinet. From it he took an enamel kidney bowl which contained a hypodermic syringe and needle, a glass ampoule and a small metal finger-saw. Using the saw he broke open the ampoule and filled the syringe with its contents. He took a wad of cotton wool, drenched it with surgical spirit and returned to the gently moaning creature on the bed.

'My friend ... my good friend ...'

'Who is that poor creature?' asked Ann.

She had allowed herself to be led from the secret part of the house which had frightened her every bit as much as the incarcerated creature itself. She sat in Lady Cranleigh's private sitting room, the glass of brandy held tightly in her still trembling hands.

'Take a little more of that!' advised the once more cool and collected dowager. Ann sipped a little of the unpleasant fiery spirit and shuddered. Lady Cranleigh looked down from the window onto the terrace thronged with her neglected guests. The band began to play again and the dancing recommenced. She looked at her future daughter-in-law, her beautiful face enigmatic.

'I want to know,' insisted Ann.

'He's a friend of the Indian.'

'That awful man with the lip?'

Lady Cranleigh left the window and moved to sit opposite

Ann. 'He's not awful,' she said patiently. 'He's a very good man ... and a very important man in his own country. The chief of his tribe.'

'Then what's he doing here?'

'George sent him.'

'George did?' Ann turned to look at a framed photograph of the ninth Marquess, the man she was to have married.

'His name is Dittar Latoni,' went on Lady Cranleigh. 'He once saved George's life, although he maintains it was George who saved his. George was grateful to Dittar and wanted me to have him here. It was the least I could do.'

'And he's happy to stay here? I don't understand.'

Lady Cranleigh sighed. 'I know. It's difficult. One needs to understand an entirely different culture. Dittar's gods are gods of retribution and atonement. When George died Dittar blamed himself. He had a need to stay here and atone for his sin ... continuing with George's spirit. For him the Venezualan jungle can no longer be his home. His gods decree against it.'

'And that poor thing locked away up there?'

'A survivor of an earlier expedition. He's thought to be German or Swiss but no identification was ever found. And when the Butiu indians did that to him they cut out his tongue. But for Dittar he would have died, but when George found them both the poor soul was already out of his mind.'

Ann took another sip of her brandy. 'How long have they been here?'

'Since George died.'

'Two years?'

'Yes.'

'Why was I never told?'

'We thought it best you shouldn't know. The fewer people the better.'

Outside the band was playing another lively quickstep accompanying the many shuffling feet on the terrace. All those guests oblivious of the secret of Cranleigh Hall. Ann closed her eyes in an attempt to shut out the thought.

'Who does know?'

'Only Charles and me.'

'The servants?'

'No. I think they may suspect, but they all knew George and loved him. They would respect his wishes as they respect his memory. It's unthinkable that Dittar and his friend should be uncared for in some institution.'

Ann looked down at her brandy suspiciously. It had burned her throat and now warmed her stomach and she felt better but she was so confused. She put the glass on the table next to her. 'Why did George keep this a secret from me? I don't understand. If you knew, why couldn't I know? We were to be married. I thought he loved me.'

Lady Cranleigh rose to pour herself a little brandy and looked with compassion on the fragile, vulnerable girl. 'Of course he loved you, child . . . in his way.'

'What d'you mean?'

'My dear, George lost his heart long before he met you . . . lost it to that filthy jungle.' Ann was startled by the sudden passion in the older woman's voice. 'It was something he shared with no one. Not with me . . . not with his brother . . . nor, my child, with you.' Lady Cranleigh drank her brandy at a gulp; something else about her that Ann found startling. It was so uncharacteristic of the woman she felt she knew. She was beginning to wonder if she knew anyone. Lady Cranleigh put down her glass and came to sit next to Ann on the sofa. She took the girl's hands in hers and held them firmly. With frank eyes she looked directly into Ann's. 'But there's something you haven't told me.'

'What's that?'

'How you came to be in the room.'

Confusion pushed in again on Ann, hurling at her fragments of a half-remembered nightmare. 'I don't know.'

'Ann. You must know.'

'I don't. I was dancing with someone. I thought at first it was that Doctor. He was dressed as Pierrot . . . the costume Charles got for him . . . but he said he wasn't.'

'Said he wasn't?'

'Yes.'

'He spoke to you?'

Ann thought for a moment. 'No, he didn't say anything. He

just kept shaking his head.'

'I see.'

'And then he started to take liberties and I got frightened. James came by and I ... ...' Total recall of the frightening incident came back to Ann with a rush. 'James! He attacked James! And he hurt him! And then I don't remember anymore except waking up in that room ... with ... with that thing.' Ann put shaking fingers to her temple which had begun to ache unbearably. She had been attacked by one man and trapped in that room by another? No! That couldn't be. And no! It couldn't be the same man. Could it have been that hideous Indian. No. There was that horrid lip. Suddenly she wanted to be with Charles. She wanted ... Lady Cranleigh's voice broke through her confusion.

'Ann, I want you to promise me something.'

'What?'

'That whatever happens you'll say nothing about the annexe or what you've seen in it.'

'I ... I ... don't know ...' Ann was hesitant, tremulous. *'Promise me!'*

There were a few guests who still dallied with the delicacies of the buffet but most had elected to rejoin the dancing. Adric was among those who dallied. He moved slowly along the line of laden tables with the plate in his hand already full to overflowing. It wasn't that Adric was greedy so much as curious: a trait that had endeared him to the Doctor. There was the widest possible variety of food to choose from and Adric's curiosity extended to all of it. He picked his way along the tables as delicately as a jungle cat in search of particularised prey. He wandered along under Brewster's benevolent eye. Brewster the butler, more royal than the king, more gracious than his employer, more jealous of his social status, watched the boy with warm amusement beneath his careful servant's mask, flattered that the repast for which he was responsible should command such devotion. As Adric drew level, Brewster proffered a dish of mousse de foies de volaille.

92

'May I tempt you to a little of this, sir?'

Adric ran curious eyes over the untouched dish, squinting suspiciously at the truffles.

'No, thanks,' he said happily. 'This'll do to be going on with.'

For the second time that evening the Pierrot descended the grand staircase in the main hall. The Doctor felt distinctly more comfortable having discarded his tail coat and was even looking forward, in some small measure, to participation in the fancy dress ball despite the cloud casting a shadow over the secret annexe and the spectre of sudden death. He wasn't to know that he was about to move under a blacker cloud, to be visited by a grimmer spectre.

The Doctor was halfway down the stairs before he saw the body of the footman lying in the hall. He hurried down the rest of the treads to stoop into a quick and expert examination of the dead man. The Doctor straightened unsteadily. Violent death was hardly new to someone of his age and experience but to have touched two corpses, both with broken necks in the space of an hour in an English country home in the year 1925, was not only beyond his experience but beyond his understanding. What on earth was going on this time?

One of the other footmen entered the hall from the direction of the kitchens and hurried towards the terrace. He saw the Doctor first and then the figure of his fellow servant. He stopped suddenly, his mouth open, unable to cope with the spectacle of an anonymous clown standing over a prostrate James and everything the sight implied. The Doctor lifted a covered hand.

'What's your name?'

'H ... Henry, sir,' stammered the unhappy footman.

'Henry, would you be good enough to tell Lord Cranleigh that there's been an accident and ask him to come here.'

'Yes, sir,' blurted Henry and started for the terrace.

'And Henry!' added the Doctor. The footman stopped.

'Yes, sir?'

'Please do it discreetly. There's no need to alarm anyone.'

Henry swallowed and pointed to his fellow.

'James, sir? He's all right? Isn't he, sir?'

'Just go and get Lord Cranleigh, there's a good fellow.'

The servant hurried on his way, flustered, frightened, fascinated. The Doctor looked down again at the body and saw, for the first time, Ann's head dress at the foot of the stairs. He picked it up, examined it in some detail and put it down on a convenient table.

7

The Doctor Stands Accused

The declining sun drove paths of gold between the wellingtonia conifers that bordered Cranleigh Park and across the trim lawns in front of the Hall. It gave added warmth and colour to the conviviality of the proceedings as the dancers' shadows lengthened on the terrace, but it brought no cheer to Lady Cranleigh's carefully composed face as she gazed sombrely down on the merriment of her guests. She turned from the window and looked at Ann.

'We'd better go down, my dear,' she said.

Henry, the footman, crossed the terrace hurriedly but unobtrusively to speak urgently to Brewster the butler, it being the butler's prerogative to communicate matters pertaining to domestic crises directly to his lordship.

Nyssa had accepted a plate from her host and was in the process of selecting delicately and modestly from the comestibles of the running buffet when she met Adric retracing his steps for another look at the gastronomical riches available. She looked with amazement and not a little embarrassment at the pile of food on Adric's plate.

'Isn't that seconds?'

Adric didn't much like her tone. 'So?'

'You pig!'

Adric sighed. 'You can only be Nyssa.'

'Just look at that!'

'You look at it!' countered Adric. 'I'm going to eat it.' And he moved off with his food in the direction of a group of guests which included Tegan, Sir Robert Muir and the Roman centurion.

Lord Cranleigh was approaching Nyssa bearing a glass of

champagne when he was intercepted by Brewster who whispered the Doctor's message relayed by Henry. Cranleigh brought the champagne to Nyssa, excused himself and made his way quickly across the terrace accompanied by Brewster and Henry.

As Adric joined her, Tegan eyed his plate with a detachment that was not without wonder. 'Have you seen the Doctor?'

'No.'

'Sure you've got enough there?'

Adric closed his eyes and summoned all his tolerance. 'Don't you start!'

Lord Cranleigh hurried across the hall to the Doctor followed by Brewster and Henry.

'Doctor?'

'I'm afraid his neck's broken,' the Doctor said quietly.

'He's dead?'

'I'm afraid so.'

'Oh, poor chap!' Lord Cranleigh knelt quickly by the body. A close look at the unfortunate footman was all the confirmation he needed. 'He must have fallen down the stairs.'

The Doctor was on the point of contradicting the statement when he remembered the presence of the servants and his promise to Lady Cranleigh. The dead man was too far away from the foot of the stairs for his neck to have been broken in a fall and the broken neck wasn't entirely without precedent. This was a case where what was called 'foul play' had to be suspected, and he had promised discretion. Lord Cranleigh straightened and turned to the butler, 'Brewster, I'm terribly sorry about this. I think, perhaps, we'd better move him to be ... well, decent.'

'Yes, milord.'

'No!' Put in the Doctor. 'I'm sorry to interrupt, Lord Cranleigh, but may I have a quiet word?' The perplexed young nobleman allowed himself to be led a little apart from the embarrassed but impassive butler and footman. 'I think it would be wise,' whispered the Doctor, 'to leave him where he is until the police get here.'

'The police?' echoed Lord Cranleigh.

'Yes.'

'Good Lord! You don't think ...?' He left the question unfinished, overcome by shock at the Doctor's implication. 'It may not be an accident,' whispered the Doctor. 'He's too far away from the stairs.'

'Good Lord,' murmured Cranleigh, aghast. He looked hard at the body and then at the waiting servants. Not an accident? Then what? And who would want to hurt James? 'All right, Brewster, thank you. That's all.' The servants turned to go. 'But please ask Sir Robert if he'll be kind enough to come here.'

'Yes, milord.'

'And not a word about this to anyone else.'

'Milord.'

The Doctor waited until they were alone before moving to the table to pick up Ann's head-dress. 'I found this on the floor.' Cranleigh took the cap and mask with the mockingly waving antennae and looked at it with mounting apprehension. 'My fiancée was wearing this,' he said. He looked at the Doctor without seeing him, his mind elsewhere, with Ann.

'I really think the police should be informed,' said the Doctor after a very long silence.

'Sir Robert will know what to do,' replied Cranleigh distractedly. 'He's not only Lord Lieutenant, he's the Chief Constable.' He turned the head-dress over and over in his hands, keeping a growing anxiety from his guest.

'In the hall?' repeated Sir Robert.

'Yes, Sir Robert,' murmured Brewster with a mammoth discretion and withdrawing quickly, implying that the Chief Constable would do well to do likewise. Sir Robert offered his apologies and withdrew accordingly. Tegan followed in his wake to join up with the abandoned Nyssa and to distance herself from the feeding Adric.

'Enjoying yourself?' asked Nyssa.

'Too right,' said Tegan. 'Seen anything of the Doctor?'

'Not for some time.'

'He's missing all the fun.'

Nyssa looked past Tegan at the group her friend had just left, her interest centred on the Centurion from whom she'd been rescued earlier. 'Who *is* that man?' she asked. Tegan turned to follow Nyssa's look. 'What man?'

'The one dressed as a soldier. That aggressive helmet and all that leather.'

'The Centurion? Oh, I don't know. I've forgotten his name but they call him Tiny for short.'

'Tiny? But he's huge.'

Tegan looked at Nyssa calculating how long it might take to explain the irony implicit in Anglo Saxon nicknames – let alone the meaning of 'nickname'. 'Don't let it worry you, Nyssa,' she said.

'What worries me is that I talked to him ... well, *he* talked to *me* ... and I didn't understand a word he said.'

'I know,' agreed Tegan. 'He's not very bright, but he *is* something of a celebrity.'

'Is he?'

'Oh, yes. He stroked Oxford home last year.'

'Stroked Oxford home?'

Tegan heard Nyssa's teeth grind together and saw her eyes cross. Too late she realised she had introduced yet another British sport that she would have to explain. As if instructing the uninitiated in the art of cricket wasn't enough, she was now stuck with making sense out of the annual Oxford and Cambridge boat race.

'Ann was wearing this.'

'Or was it the other one?' asked Sir Robert.

'No,' insisted Lord Cranleigh. 'Nyssa's out on the terrace. I've just left her. This is Ann's.'

Sir Robert Muir looked from the incongruous Pierrot, whom he now knew to be the Doctor, to the Marquess's anxious face. 'I shouldn't worry, Charles, she can't be far. Let's look for her.'

Lord Cranleigh's eyes rested sightlessly on his friend's concerned face. He turned to the Doctor. 'Where was she when you last saw her?'

'I haven't seen her,' were the muffled words behind the painted mask.

'You were dancing with her.'

'I was?'

'Or was it the other one?' suggested Sir Robert.

'No. *I* was dancing with Nyssa.'

'Doctor?' Sir Robert's eyes bored into the Pierrot mask. Embarrassment made the Doctor feel suddenly very hot. He removed his head piece revealing a flushed, apologetic smile. 'I'm sorry, I haven't danced with anyone. I've only just come down from upstairs.'

The concern on Sir Robert's face deepened and he looked long and hard at the Doctor before speaking. 'But I saw you, sir.'

'You *saw* me?'

'Yes. You danced with one or other of the young ladies from the terrace into the drawing room. I saw you.'

The Doctor smiled broadly as the only possible explanation of Sir Robert's statement came readily to mind. He turned from one to the other of them. 'You saw *me*?' he asked. 'Or this?' He replaced his head piece thus losing all identity.

'Well, yes. That,' admitted Sir Robert.

'Then what you saw,' the Pierrot announced triumphantly, 'was someone dressed in an identical costume.' And the Doctor turned to Lord Cranleigh for confirmation of this.

'That is the only costume of its kind,' said Cranleigh bleakly.

Another surge of embarrassment sent the Doctor's temperature climbing but, this time, he left the head piece where it was since it was more comfortable to cover his confusion.

The only costume of its kind? His mind chased about for an alternative explanation but, whichever way it turned, any illuminating thought remained light years ahead of it. Sir Robert's mouth had set in a thin line. 'Would you please tell us why you deny being with Miss Talbot?'

'I can only repeat that I've not laid eyes on her since the end of the cricket,' said the harrassed Doctor.

'That's just not good enough, sir.'

Again the Doctor looked from one to the other. 'Is this some sort of joke?'

'That, sir,' said Sir Robert, pointing to the body of the footman, 'is hardly a joke.'

The Doctor was grateful his mask hid the hot flush that he felt burn his cheeks at the monstrous accusation. 'You can't think I had anything to do with that!' The tacit response to his protest confirmed to him that they did indeed think he had something to do with that. He turned on Lord Cranleigh. 'Please, may I make a suggestion?'

'What is it?'

'Find Miss Talbot and ask her. She'll confirm that what I say is true.'

His lordship's pale blue eyes had taken on a steely look. They were fixed upon the Doctor with an implacability rare in the Time Lord's experience. The eyes that had earlier acknowledged a hero now accused him of villainy. Worse was yet to come.

'That is precisely what I intend to do,' said Lord Cranleigh tightly. 'And I ask you to stay here and not attempt to leave.'

'Of course,' groaned the hapless Doctor. He couldn't begin to calculate the effect it would have if he announced the existence of another dead body in the house. Without the presence of Lady Cranleigh it was hardly likely to lift suspicion from him.

'That's him!'

All heads turned towards the shout; to the half-landing where the treads divided and ascended separately to the floor above. Lady Cranleigh stood there with Ann. Cranleigh bounded up the stairs to them.

'Darling! Are you all right?'

'Oh, Charles!'

Ann relaxed in her fiancé's arms seeking comfort, some order from the chaos of shock and confusion she'd suffered for the past hour. Over Cranleigh's shoulder she looked down at the Pierrot again. 'That's who attacked me!'

'Attacked you!'

Cranleigh pushed her a little apart from him the better to study her. 'Are you hurt?'

'No.' Ann saw the body on the hall floor with the realisation that James had not been moved from the spot where she remembered seeing him fall. 'Oh, Charles! Something dreadful's happening! I'm so confused.' She pointed at the Doctor. '*He* did that to James! Who is he?'

The Doctor felt an unbearable prickling at the back of his neck as the adrenalin was pumped through his bloodstream by both hearts going full pelt. He removed his head piece. 'It's only me,' he said with an uncharacteristic humility brought on by total mystification.

'It *was* you,' said Ann without surprise.

'Only me,' repeated the Doctor innocently.

'Oh, how awful!' gasped Ann, in the grip of a sickening loathing that she should have been the victim of someone whose earlier credentials should be so beyond reproach as to be positively saint-like. Far from confirming his innocence, Ann Talbot had joined the Doctor's accusers to the frightening extent of pointing him out as James's murderer.

'Look here,' he began, with no conspicuous confidence, 'you're all making a big mistake. I'm every bit as confused as Miss Talbot, I can tell you.'

'Charles!' called Lady Cranleigh sharply as her son started back down the stairs. Cranleigh stopped and his mother drew level with him. 'Please take this carefully,' she said softly and for his ears alone. 'Ann has had a very great shock, and I mean,' she slowed her words for great emphasis, ' ... a ... very ... great shock.'

Cranleigh looked back anxiously at Ann. It was perfectly apparent that his mother was entirely right. He could see, even from this distance, that the girl was still trembling violently. He turned back, caught his mother's anxious eye, and moved down the stairs to the Doctor.

'Well? You heard Miss Talbot.'

'Yes,' said the Doctor as evenly as he could. 'I heard Miss Talbot and I can only repeat that she's mistaken.'

'I'm not mistaken!' Ann almost shouted, coming down to

join Lady Cranleigh. 'He danced with me and then pulled me in here. I shouted for help and James came and he did that to him! He killed him!'

'Oh, I say,' murmured the Doctor, 'this really is a bit thick, you know. It's perfectly obvious to me that Miss Talbot is mistaking me for someone else wearing exactly the same costume.'

'And it's perfectly obvious to me that there is no other costume and that you're lying,' replied Cranleigh as calmly as he could since he was fighting an irresistible urge to thrash this cricket-playing blackguard within an inch of his life.

'I've made it a life-long habit never to tell a lie,' said the Doctor with hauteur.

'A veritable George Washington,' sneered Lord Cranleigh. The Doctor decided to ignore the jibe and to pursue his defence on another tack. 'May I ask Miss Talbot a question?'

'You may not!'

'Charles!' interceded Sir Robert in his rôle as Chief Constable. 'It can do no harm.'

Cranleigh looked at his fiancée who now had Lady Cranleigh's arm about her and appeared to have recovered some of her composure. 'Very well. Ask your question!'

'Thank you,' murmured the Doctor politely. He looked up at Ann and was not encouraged to see that she shrank from him a little. 'Miss Talbot,' he began, 'did you hear my voice? Did I say anything to you?'

'No.'

'Did you see my face?'

'No.'

'Then what it comes down to is that you danced with this costume, you were brought in here by this costume, and you were attacked by this costume. Would you agree to that?'

Confusion returned to Ann with a rush. She'd not seen her attacker's face and she'd not heard him speak and she was still striving to come to terms with finding herself with that hideous, pathetic creature in the room with the iron bars at the window. Her mouth opened but it voiced no answer.

'Wait a bit, wait a bit!' put in Cranleigh a little belatedly.

'Ann, he must have asked you to dance.'

Ann thought for a moment and then shook her head.

'He didn't ask you?'

'No. He ... he just held out a hand.'

The Doctor looked at them all in turn with an expression of undisguised triumph, seeking to persuade his audience that his minor point was a major advantage. 'If there is some doubt I think I deserve the benefit of it,' he said with an attempt at modesty that fell little short of smugness.

'You'll get what you deserve,' said the young nobleman darkly, with his instincts still bent on retribution for the abuse offered his beloved. But doubt now clouded his face. Could there possibly be another costume like the one he'd found in the attic? No! He'd seen this man dancing with Ann and so had Robert. A duplication of the costume wasn't possible. They were bound to have seen it. He looked at Sir Robert. 'Shall you or I telephone the station?'

The Doctor was in no doubt about which station Lord Cranleigh had in mind. His educated guess was that he was about to be arrested and this called for the exposure of a potential skeleton in a Cranleigh Hall cupboard. He'd make no bones about it. Lady Cranleigh and her South American Indian guest would substantiate his claim of innocence concerning the other broken neck.

'Lady Cranleigh,' began the Doctor, but the lady in question cut in sharply, moving quickly down the stairs towards the body of the footman. 'Charles, shouldn't you ...' She gestured delicately at the embarrassment presented by the corpse.

'No, Madge,' interrupted Sir Robert smoothly, 'not until the police get here.'

'But you *are* the police,' protested Lady Cranleigh.

'Precisely,' responded Sir Robert. 'And that makes it imperative that Sergeant Markham and Doctor Hathaway both be here before the body is moved.'

Lady Cranleigh took refuge from the Doctor with a display of social outrage. 'But my guests ...!' Sir Robert took his cue and took control. He looked directly at his host. 'Charles, I suggest you call it a day. Tell your guests there's been an accident and ask them to leave. But first, ring the station. Tell them what's happened.' He flicked a look at the Doctor and then at Lady Cranleigh. 'Tell them there's been an accident and ask them to send Doctor Hathaway.'

The Doctor watched Lady Cranleigh's clenched hands relax. Her son moved off quickly and then turned back to look at the Doctor. 'What about him?'

'Leave everything to me please, Charles.'

'Righto.'

Sir Robert waited for Cranleigh to go and then looked at the two women on the stairs. 'Madge?'

'I wish to remain, Robert,' said Lady Cranleigh.

'As you please,' said the knight formally and directed his attention at the Doctor. 'Well, sir? Is all this the reason why you wished to remain incognito?'

'No, it isn't,' said the Doctor with a controlled impatience.

'Then perhaps you'll be good enough to tell me your name.'

'You already know my name.'

'You are known only as the Doctor.'

'That's right.'

'Doctor who?'

'If you will.'

Sir Robert sighed. There would obviously be no profit from this line of enquiry. 'Have you any means of indentification?' he asked.

'No. I've never needed any.'

'Fortunate man,' rejoined Sir Robert wryly. 'But you say that you're from Guy's Hospital and that you were sent here by Doctor Handicombe as a replacement player in today's match.'

'I never said any such thing,' corrected the Doctor.

'But Handicome did send you?'

'No. You all assumed he had.'

'Then why didn't you deny it?'

'I don't know.'

'You don't know?'

'Yes, all right. I do know. I couldn't resist the game of cricket.'

Sir Robert frowned. He was deeply worried that such an

exemplary cricketer appeared not to have an exemplary character to match. It denied a whole code of ethics, contradicted a whole way of life. 'Then you weren't sent here?'

The Time Lord hesitated. The question had to be answered truthfully and it wouldn't be the first time that the Grand Council on Gallifrey had seen fit to nudge the TARDIS towards moral intervention. He remembered the Master's attempt to topple King John of England. 'It's possible I might have been.'

'You might have been?'

'Let's say I'm here by accident . . . by chance.'

'By chance? You and your friends . . . or perhaps I should call them accomplices?' Sir Robert had been reminded suddenly of the uncanny coincidence presented by the appearance of Nyssa. What if it was no coincidence? What if it was some diabolical foreign plot . . . some anarchist plot to substitute a double for Ann and infiltrate the House of Lords? It wasn't all that far-fetched. He recalled that fellow Winston Churchill, when he was Home Secretary, directing the siege of Sidney Street. Those people had been anarchists led by Peter the Painter who had subsequently disappeared. The whole puzzling affair had never been satisfactorily explained and this Doctor and his accomplices, with the exception of the girl Tegan who said she was Australian, had been deliberately vague about their place of origin. Where was Traken? What was an Alzarian? 'By chance?' he repeated. 'You're all here by chance?'

'Yes,' replied the Doctor evenly, 'but I'd be grateful if you'd leave my friends out of this.'

'I see. Then you agree that whatever "this" is . . . you're in it?'

The Doctor sighed deeply and looked at Lady Cranleigh who avoided his eyes. He was in it, all right. In it up to his neck. The distant band stopped playing abruptly in mid-number. Lord Cranleigh would now be on the terrace making an appeal to his guests among whom was the murderer of James . . . and of Digby? The Doctor was powerless to prevent the guests from dispersing. He was not only bound by his word to Lady Cranleigh; he doubted his capacity to influence Sir Robert in any action since he was unquestionably under suspicion. 'By chance,' mused Sir Robert. 'But you are a doctor of medicine?'

'Among other things.'

'What other things?'

'My doctorate extends to mathematics, moral philosophy and history,' said the Doctor modestly. The statement was impressive but, to his listeners, hardly more credible than his protestations of innocence.

'And what, may I ask, is such a person doing here by chance?' persisted Sir Robert. There was no escape for the Doctor. He just had to go on giving truthful answers to awkward questions until the inevitable declaration of his fantastic identity would plunge him into the deepest possible hot water.

'I'm very much afraid that if I tell you . . . you won't believe me.'

'Without a doubt, if you go on telling lies. But you're going to have to give account of yourself sooner or later and I must remind you that I'm the Lord Lieutenant of this county *and* the Chief Constable and that you, sir, are under suspicion of murder.'

The Doctor drew a deep breath. 'I'm a Time Lord.'

Sir Robert blinked and looked at the two women on the stairs. 'You're a *what*?'

'I told you,' the Doctor grimaced.

'I think you'd better try again.'

'I travel in space and time,' the Doctor groaned on. ' . . . I have a time-machine . . .' He ground to a halt as he saw Sir Robert's lip curl, and then became inspired as an aspect of English literature surfaced in his memory. 'Perhaps you may have read H. G. Wells.'

Sir Robert's lips continued to curl into a convolution of derisive disbelief before they opened to announce: 'I *know* H. G. Wells. He writes fiction.'

The implication in the last word and the honed edge on Sir Robert's voice were not lost on the unhappy Doctor. There was only one way of combatting disbelief in the TARDIS and that was to expose it to vulgar gaze, to demonstrate it. But the TARDIS was at Cranleigh Halt railway station and the Chief Constable was not going to be persuaded into an unnecessary visit to a police box. The thought crossed his troubled mind that he could produce its Servicing Certificate which recorded all services and modifications in its long history and his hand was halfway to his breast pocket before he remembered that his tail coat was upstairs in his room. In any case the document was computer software and just as incredible to the feudal forces of 1925 England as a time-machine. There was nothing for it but to enlist the aid of Lady Cranleigh and expose the existence of the other body, however distasteful.

'I'm sorry, Lady Cranleigh . . .'

'Sorry, Doctor?' Her eyes were wide and her head held high. It came suddenly to the Doctor that she must now suspect him of Digby's death also. After all, he couldn't prove that he'd arrived here only this afternoon. He turned to the Chief Constable. 'There's something you should know, Sir Robert.'

'Yes?'

The Doctor turned to look at Lady Cranleigh before continuing. She returned the look without faltering, her eyes outstaring his. He pointed to the body of the footman. 'This poor man isn't the only victim. There's another body.'

'Another body?' Sir Robert looked involuntarily at Lady Cranleigh.

'A servant called Digby,' said the Doctor.

'Digby?' The name was clearly unknown to Sir Robert who glanced again at the impassive Lady Cranleigh.

'He's in the annexe.'

'Annexe? What annexe?' Sir Robert turned to his hostess. 'Madge?' Lady Cranleigh said nothing, her eyes still directly holding those of the Doctor. In the distance the guests could be heard departing, and departing quietly in consideration of the circumstances that had broken up a festive occasion. A few motor-car doors and receding engines were the only distinctive sounds.

'There's a secret annexe,' said the Doctor quietly.

'A secret annexe? Madge?' repeated Sir Robert, turning to Lady Cranleigh for confirmation.

The dowager Marchioness looked at her perplexed questioner with a monumental calm before directing her statement at the Doctor. 'Like Mr Wells, the gentleman appears to have a vivid imagination.'

The Doctor was ill prepared for what, for him, was an act of arrant betrayal. He found it difficult to believe his ears but, shocked as he was, the startled look that Ann threw at the older woman wasn't lost on him. Neither was it lost on Lady Cranleigh. Ann looked back at the Doctor and glimpsed him in a new light. Here was another who knew of the annexe. Was her future mother-in-law going to deny its existence?

'The annexe I'm talking about isn't in my imagination but in my experience,' the Doctor managed at last.

'I understood you to be talking about a body,' said Lady Cranleigh distantly. The Doctor no longer had any compunction about offending the susceptibilities of this woman so clearly aligned against him. 'I showed you the body of a man called Digby hidden in a cupboard.'

'Did you?' The eyes were cold and fixed.

'I showed it to you and the Indian.'

Sir Robert was startled. 'The Indian?'

'A South American Indian,' went on the Doctor implacably. 'I've forgotten his name but he has a protruding lower lip ... achieved under traction with a plate. It's a characteristic of some tribes. Once seen, never forgotten.'

The statement was so bizarre, so altogether outlandish that it robbed Sir Robert of speech. He remembered that the girl Tegan had talked about seeing such a being, but perhaps this was another of the gang. The dumbfounded knight looked at Lady Cranleigh for some enlightenment but she remained silent. Ann caught her breath, suspecting that Lady Cranleigh was dissembling, but unable to confirm the existence of the Indian without being disloyal. And what about this other body? She longed to be able to unburden her confusion on the solid Sir Robert, to confide in him the secret of the annexe. Her loyalty was strained to its limits at the mention of another body. Lady Cranleigh remained silent.

'Body in a cupboard?' muttered an acutely uncomfortable Sir Robert. 'Indian with a lip?' The Doctor decided that attack was now the only defence. He would take the battle into the enemy camp. 'With Lady Cranleigh's permission I'm prepared to show you.' The Doctor was confident he could make his way back to the annexe now that he'd been shown the mechanisms that activated the panels.

'Madge?' murmured Sir Robert tentatively.

'By all means,' responded Lady Cranleigh unexpectedly.

Anything further was interrupted by the arrival of her son from the direction of the drawing room.

'Everybody's going,' he announced and nodded towards the Doctor. 'Except his friends. I've got them in the drawing room ... with Henry keeping an eye on them until the Sergeant gets here.'

Anger suddenly erupted in the good Doctor. He'd taken enough, and for his companions to be treated with such contumely was the last straw. 'I refuse to be talked to like a criminal any longer,' he said loudly. 'There's something terribly wrong here that calls for a thorough investigation and I call on Sir Robert Muir to see that it's carried out.'

The outburst took everyone a little by surprise, most of all Lord Cranleigh who was ignorant of all that had led up to it. 'What's he getting at?' he asked Sir Robert.

'Oh, some cock and bull story about a body in an annexe.'

Cranleigh was suddenly rigid, a fact that didn't escape the notice of his mother or his fiancée or, for that matter, the Doctor.

'It's not a cock and bull story,' the Doctor said with justified belligerence. 'There's a body in your secret annexe, Lord Cranleigh, and I demand the right to show it to Sir Robert.'

'A what? A body?'

'Yes!'

'Oh!' suddenly cried Ann. It was an opening Lady Cranleigh had been waiting for and she seized it. 'Charles,' she said, 'Look after Ann! She's very upset. I can deal with all this nonsense.' She steered Ann into the arms of her son and, at the touch of comfort, the girl began to sob. Lady Cranleigh turned to Sir Robert. 'Well, Robert? Shall we go?' The knight wriggled uncomfortably. He couldn't remember a more embarrassing time. All this was very much against the grain. *Very* much against the grain.

'Very well,' he said.

Lady Cranleigh turned to the Doctor. 'Would you be good enough to lead the way?' she asked with cool politeness. The Doctor nodded curtly and preceded her and Sir Robert up the stairs watched by the sorely troubled tenth Marquess who held a confused and miserable Ann in his arms and a tormenting secret in his heart.

The Doctor led the way along the main corridor on the second floor and stopped by a familiar section of panelling. Unerringly his fingers found the protuberance in the carving that activated the secret door. He stood aside, tacitly inviting Lady Cranleigh to precede him and then indicating that Sir Robert should follow. Bringing up the rear he joined the others in the corridor from which rose the steps to the room in the tower. He turned to Sir Robert. 'This is the annexe. Up there ...' he gestured towards the steps, ' ... is a room with bars on the window.'

'This is one of the largest existing priest holes in the country,' elaborated Lady Cranleigh for Sir Robert's benefit. 'The room at the top of the steps is the royal chamber. The bars on the window were for added protection.'

Not to be outdone, the Doctor showed Sir Robert the bathroom and then moved to the further bed-sitting room and tapped on the door. There being no response he opened the door and stepped into the room. Sir Robert followed him wonderingly, overcome by these revelations. He'd known the Cranleighs all his life without dreaming this place existed. 'This, I suspect,' said the Doctor, 'is the room used by the Indian. That gramophone record is Portugese.'

Sir Robert moved to the machine. There was no longer a record on the turntable and all the other records had been removed. 'There's no record here,' he said. The Doctor looked at Lady Cranleigh whose eyes were averted. 'Then he's been here since I was here,' he said unabashedly and led the way to the next room, taking note of Lady Cranleigh's imperturbable calm.

'I'm convinced that this room,' began the Doctor as he opened the door, 'was occupied by a man called Raymond Digby ... now dead, as you will see.' He looked about the room with surprised eyes. All evidence of recent habitation had been removed. There were no books or magazines. The bed had been stripped to its mattress and dust sheets covered the other items of furniture. The wardrobe door, from which had hung the short white coat, was now closed. The Doctor looked at Lady Cranleigh who stared directly ahead of her with complete lack of interest in the room or its contents. The Doctor walked to the wardrobe and opened it. Empty. He knew it would be empty even before he opened the doors, for the mystery of Cranleigh Hall had moved into the sinister area of conspiracy.

'Doesn't look very lived-in to me,' observed Sir Robert. He looked at Lady Cranleigh who answered his unspoken question with quiet dignity.

'I've not been in this room for years,' she said. 'I can't remember the last time.'

In spite of himself the Doctor felt a grudging admiration for this, his latest opponent: this woman whose strength he'd seriously underestimated. He wondered how she would cope with the impact of his ultimate revelation. With a courtly gesture he invited her to lead the way from the room. In the corridor she stopped, awaiting the Doctor's next move.

The Doctor advanced on the next secret panel followed by the others. Again his fingers were instantly on target and the rear of the cupboard in the parallel corridor slid back with the noiseless ease of recent use. The Doctor lost no time in moving through to the adjoining corridor and along it to the cupboard at the far end. He waited for the others to join him and then, with his eyes on Lady Cranleigh, indicated the door handle. 'The body's behind this door.'

Lady Cranleigh looked at Sir Robert who, after a moment's hesitation, stepped forward to grasp the handle. He moved back swinging the door with him and exposing the interior of the cupboard to the evening sunlight filtering through the skylights.

With instant realisation the Doctor saw that he had been outwitted. In place of Digby's body was a large doll; a small girl dressed in the fashion of a generation earlier. Lady Cranleigh was in no hurry to press home her advantage. She looked directly at the Doctor's discomforture, her fine features enigmatic.

'My father gave me that when I was six,' she said serenely.

8

Under Arrest

Lord Cranleigh held the still trembling Ann tightly in his
arms, his mind in turmoil. He desperately wanted to be with
the others in the annexe, to learn the identity of the body
there, but Ann was too terrified for him to leave her and too
vulnerable because of her blissful ignorance of Cranleigh
Hall's closely guarded secret.

'Oh, Charles, Charles,' she sobbed, 'why couldn't you have
told me before? All this time! And to have found out like that!
How could you?'

'There, darling,' he murmured protectively, 'everything's
going to be all right. Everything was for the best. It was the
way mother wanted it, and the way George wanted it. We
didn't want to frighten you.'

'That poor creature!'

'Was he ill?' Cranleigh's eyes were haunted as he waited for
her answer.

'Ill? I don't know ... he was so ... so ...' She broke down
again and Cranleigh's arms tightened about her. He waited
for her sobs to ease and then said very gently, 'You haven't
told me how you got into that room.'

'I don't know. I suppose it was that man ... that Doctor ...
who took me.'

'No,' contradicted Cranleigh, 'He had no reason to.'

'Then I don't know. Oh, Charles!' The young nobleman's
sorrowing face was furrowed with painful thought. What he'd
just learned from his fraught fiancée pointed the finger of
suspicion away from the Doctor but then, at whom? There
was a gap in what he knew that needed desperately to be filled
and there was an imposed limit on what he could learn from

the suffering girl in his arms. Perhaps he could find out more about this mysterious Doctor elsewhere. He gently detached himself from Ann.

'Where are you going?'

'Just to make a telephone call.'

'Don't leave me!'

'There's no need for that, my dear. Come with me!'

With a comforting arm about her he guided her across the hall and into the book-lined study where he consulted a directory and picked up the ear piece of the telephone. 'Sit down,' he said gently. 'This won't take long,' and then into the mouthpiece, 'London Bridge 2000, please.'

Ann sat forward on the edge of a deep leather arm chair like a frightened bird poised for flight while Cranleigh waited to be connected with Guy's Hospital in London. He announced his identity to a distant, distorted voice and asked to speak to Doctor Handicombe. Very soon he was listening to a warm apology from the doctor who had only just heard that the colleague he'd sent as a replacement for the Cranleigh XI had caught the wrong connection and had finished up in Glasgow. He was deeply sorry and hoped the day hadn't been disastrous. With mixed feelings Cranleigh passed on the news of the resounding victory to be answered by the distant voice declaring diagnostically that it was an ill wind that blew nobody any good. The disturbed nobleman hung up the ear piece no better informed about the identity of his mysterious visitor and still trying to piece together the frightening fragments of the day. What progressively bothered him was this Doctor's lack of motive for attacking Ann, his talk of a body and his silence about what had terrified Ann in the annexe. Ann searched Cranleigh's taut face. 'What did he say?' she asked anxiously.

'Nothing of any help.'

Ann tried to control her trembling lips and tears again brimmed in her eyes. Cranleigh moved quickly to comfort her with encircling arms.

Sir Robert Muir watched the Doctor change out of his

114

incriminating costume with the detachment of the senior police officer performing an unpleasant duty. He had insisted on being present for the obvious reason that, left alone, his prime suspect would undoubtedly abscond. The man had proved himself an intelligent and skilful athlete and he was taking no chances.

The Doctor picked up his tail coat and looked across at the secret panel by the bed now obdurately closed. 'I suppose it's no use telling you that a panel over there was open and that I went through it and it closed behind me?'

'No,' was the laconic answer.

'And that I was away from here for some time and that anyone could have come in and taken that.' The Doctor pointed to the Pierrot costume on the bed.

'And brought it back again?'

'Yes.'

'Who?'

'I don't know who.' The Doctor couldn't help ponder how unimaginative policemen were. Or perhaps it was a case of saturation with preposterous alibis and lurid red herrings. In either case his prospects didn't look good and were not likely to improve unless new evidence came to light, like a very dead body. Lady Cranleigh was a force to be reckoned with. His worst fears were endorsed by an officially urbane Chief Constable. 'You've made some very wild statements entirely without substantiation. And now, if you're quite ready, we'll go below and wait for Sergeant Markham.'

Dittar Latoni, Chief of the Utubi, looked up from his book in response to the light tapping on the stout door. He glanced over his shoulder at his charge, still unconscious on the bed, the hideous features softened by the warm glow of the setting sun slanting through the barred window. The Indian put down his book, rose from the desk, and took the heavy key from his pocket with which to open the door.

He saw, without surprise, the erect figure of Lady Cranleigh on the landing and slipped through the door to join her. The dowager Marchioness gripped the Indian's arm.

'Thank you, Dittar,' she said warmly, 'You have done well. But now, if we're to save your friend, we must do better.'

'I'm getting a bit fed up with this,' muttered Adric.

'Join the club,' said Tegan with feeling, looking at the unfortunate Henry who was mounting reluctant guard of them in the drawing room. 'But we wait for the Doctor.'

'But where is he?' asked Nyssa plaintively.

'Perhaps *he's* the accident.' Adric's tone was sepulchral as he put an empty plate down on a nearby table.

'Think yourself lucky it's not you,' added Tegan drily. 'You could go pop at any minute.'

Adric was on the point of expostulation when the Doctor appeared in the custody of Sir Robert. Tegan rose to meet them. 'Oh, you're all right,' she said with relief.

'I'm not all right,' responded the Doctor. 'I've been arrested.'

'Arrested?' echoed Tegan.

'And charged with murder.'

'Murder?'

'And it's very nearly as bad to have everything I say repeated,' complained the Doctor irritably.

'Don't be silly!' said Nyssa.

'And I'm not being silly!' snapped the Doctor.

'I don't mean you. I mean the whole situation is silly.'

'Tell that to Sir Robert!' said the Doctor, as before.

'And that goes for the three of us,' added Tegan. She looked squarely at Sir Robert. 'The Doctor's quite incapable of any such act. A pig would find it easier to fly than the Doctor to murder anyone.'

'Yes!' agreed Nyssa hotly.

'Yes!' said Adric with vigour.

The Doctor was warmed by his companions' emphatic loyalty. He was even able to manage a small smile. As for Sir Robert there was an area of his heart that wanted to believe the declarations but his mind had to be involved here, and involved professionally, and facts were facts.

'Your friend has failed to give a good account of himself,'

he said sombrely, 'and in the circumstances that leaves me with no alternative but to take him into custody for questioning.'

'Why can't you question him here?' asked Tegan crossly.

Lady Cranleigh entered from the hall followed by two uniformed policemen. Sergeant Markham was a ruddy-faced country-man approaching middle-age and of bucolic proportions, and the young constable was clearly overawed by the situation and the surroundings.

'Enquiries will have to be made,' answered Sir Robert, 'concerning background and identity. Let's hope that the truth of this tragic matter will emerge in the course of those enquiries.'

'Let's hope so indeed,' agreed the Doctor with feeling, his eyes on Lady Cranleigh who returned his look boldly with no hint of shame. Sir Robert turned to the policemen.

'Ah, Markham. I expected you earlier.'

'. . . I was over at Chiddleton, Sir Robert,' said the Sergeant. 'Young Cooper in trouble again. Poaching. I had to sort that out. Doctor Hathaway's taking a look at the body,' he added with confidential relish.

'Good! I'm arresting this gentleman, Sergeant, on suspicion of murder.'

'Very good, sir.'

The young constable looked at his superior in anticipation of an order. For a moment it looked as though the Sergeant would lick his lips. No charge of murder had been brought hereabouts in living memory. Sir Robert turned back to the Doctor. 'And I must warn you, sir, that anything you say will be taken down and may be given in evidence.'

'Very kind of you,' said the Doctor watching both policemen search diligently for notebook and pencil, 'but I prefer to say nothing for the moment.' Sir Robert looked pointedly at the Sergeant and both policemen dutifully noted the accused's statement. The Sergeant then put away his notebook and produced a pair of handcuffs. The Doctor looked directly at the unrepentant Lady Cranleigh and held out his wrists.

'I hardly think that will be necessary,' said Sir Robert

uncomfortably, 'but I shall prefer the charge personally at the station, Sergeant.'

'Very good, Sir Robert.'

'The Doctor may be saying nothing,' announced Tegan stepping forward purposefully, 'but I have something to say.'

The policemen felt for their notebooks.

'If you arrest him you must also arrest the three of us.'

'No,' said the Doctor quickly.

'Yes,' said Tegan severely.

Sir Robert blinked and looked at the Doctor's companions in turn, 'On what charge?'

'The same charge. We're his accomplices.'

'Accomplices?'

'Or would it be better to call us accessories?' There was no doubt about the determination in Tegan's eyes and Sir Robert had to consider that her statement, in front of witnesses, was tantamount to a confession. 'Very well,' he said. He turned to the policemen and the portly Sergeant looked discomforted. 'Transportation's going to be a bit difficult, Sir Robert,' he ventured.

'No, it isn't,' declared Lady Cranleigh without hesitation. 'The Rolls is at your disposal, Sergeant Markham, and so is Tanner.'

'Thank you, milady.'

From the moment of Tegan's intervention the Doctor's eyes hadn't left Lady Cranleigh. He now knew that she must know the identity of the murderer and was protecting him. He also knew that she must be a woman of conscience and, therefore, susceptible to the horror of injustice and the suffering of the innocent. He was convinced it was but a matter of time before her resolve was undermined by finer feelings, but what still troubled him was his inability to reason the motive for her course of action. He wasn't to know, that in this case, desperation was the enemy of logic. As it was the dowager Marchioness returned the Doctor's penetrating look imperturbably.

Sir Robert indicated to Markham that it was time to leave and the Sergeant responded not uncheerfully, 'Come along, there, please.'

The Doctor stopped in front of his erstwhile hostess with the intention of bringing more moral pressure to bear. He smiled charmingly and said quietly and without irony, 'Thank you, Lady Cranleigh, for a delightfully unexpected day.'

Lady Cranleigh's fine-boned features remained inscrutable.

The Rolls-Royce bowled sedately along evening-shaded lanes towards the police station in Upper Cranleigh, followed respectfully by the 1923 bull-nosed Morris-Cowley that did duty for a police car. The Sergeant had elected to drive the suspects and had promoted his junior to share the Rolls with Sir Robert and Doctor Hathaway, a local general practioner and part-time police surgeon who had confirmed that James, the footman, had died from a broken neck that was not, in his considered opinion, the result of an accident. The elderly medico kept his own counsel and his eyes on the road ahead doing his best not to feel self-conscious about sharing the Cranleigh Rolls with a uniformed policeman and a Chief Constable attired as an eighteen-century buck.

Nyssa shared the front of the Morris-Cowley with Sergeant Markham, something on which the worthy police officer had insisted, while crammed together in the back were the Doctor, Tegan and Adric. Adric looked at the Doctor who was plunged so deep in thought that it defied interruption. The young Alzarian turned to Tegan. 'What's an accessory?'

Tegan thought before she answered. 'Someone who shares in a crime.'

'And we're that?'

'We are now. Yes.'

'What do they do to murderers?'

Tegan thought again, remembering they were in the England of 1925. 'Hang them,' she said gloomily, adding, 'But not you. You're under age.'

'What will they do to me, then?'

'Shut you up until you're twenty-one, and then hang you.'

Adric's eyes widened in disbelief. 'But that's barbaric!'

'Yes,' agreed Tegan. 'And if you happened to be ill you'd be nursed back to health and then hanged.'

'But that's illogical!'

'Think yourself lucky! If we'd got here a hundred years earlier we'd be packed off to my country.'

'What for?'

'Hard labour and not a lot to eat.'

'Then we've got to do something about this.'

Tegan looked at the Doctor who sat between them, apparently unaware of the conversation. He's at it again, she thought, he's gone conveniently into hiding.

'Doctor!'

The Doctor was lost in another world, the secret world of Cranleigh Hall and the occupied annexe. Tegan had the temerity to nudge him in the ribs, a display of disrespect which appeared to go unnoticed but which had the desired effect of dragging him back into a world which included imminent incarceration in Upper Cranleigh police station.

'Doctor?'

'What is it?'

'I think Adric has a good point,' said Tegan from a great height.

'What's that?'

'He thinks we've got to do something about this.'

'Very good thinking!' said the Doctor equably. 'That's just what we're doing.'

'I was under the distinct impression that we're on our way to the lock-up.'

'To have this whole business investigated.' He watched Tegan heave a heavy sigh, close her eyes and purse her lips. 'What's the alternative?'

Tegan opened her eyes, looked to see that the Sergeant's interest wasn't on them via the rear mirror and hissed, 'Get to the TARDIS and get out of here.'

The Doctor turned to Tegan, his eyes large with innocence and said blandly, 'We can't do that.'

'Why not?'

'It would be cowardly.'

'Cowardly?'

'There are people in trouble here.'

'Yes! Us!'

'No, at Cranleigh Hall. You don't want that on your conscience, do you, like Lady Cranleigh?'

'What's Lady Cranleigh got to do with it?'

The Doctor smiled widely at the short-tempered Tegan: the smile that she had come to know meant even deeper immersion in an already deadly dangerous enterprise. 'Lady Cranleigh's bent on hiding something,' he said. 'And I'm bent on finding out what she's bent on hiding.'

'You're just bent,' Tegan muttered to herself.

'But you, too, have a point,' said the Doctor, by way of compensation for committing his companions to a personal danger. Although he'd rejected the idea of flight in the TARDIS his feud with Lady Cranleigh had put from his mind the use of the TARDIS to establish his identity. He leaned forward. 'Sergeant Markham?'

'Yes, sir?' This was England where the malefactor was considered innocent until proven guilty and, therefore, not deprived of status or title. Besides, the miscreant had had the goodness to address him by name.

'Would you be good enough to stop at the station?'

'We shall be stopping at the station, sir.'

'I mean the railway station.'

The portly police sergeant was aware of his cerebral limitations. His wife was never slow to point out that if he'd had any brains he'd be an inspector by now, but he resented the assumption from the back seat that he was stupid enough to aid and abet dangerous criminals in a bid for liberty.

'I'm sorry, sir, I can't do that.'

'Why not?'

'Not without the authority of the Chief Constable, sir. I'd have to ask, Sir Robert.'

'Then ask him.'

'He's in the car in front, sir,' said the Sergeant stolidly.

'Then give him a toot on your horn.'

'Can't do that, sir.'

'Why not?'

'Not my place to, sir.'

'That presents no problem,' said the Doctor. 'We'll do it for you. Adric, you're nearest.' Adric needed no further encouragement. He leaned over the policeman's shoulder, grasped the rubber bulb of the horn and tweaked it twice. Clusters of roosting birds flew, frightened, out of the overhanging trees. The Sergeant slapped indignantly at Adric's hand. 'Don't do that!'

The Doctor glanced ahead at the unhesitant Rolls and countermanded the order with a nodding head and a stabbing index finger. Braving the slapping hand Adric pounced on the horn again. Sir Robert looked back at the following police car and bent forward to talk to Tanner. The Rolls slowed to a stop.

Tegan wanted to hug the Doctor but contented herself with clapping her hands in silent applause. The Morris-Cowley pulled up behind the Rolls and the Doctor leapt out with the Sergeant in frantic, rolling pursuit. Drawing level with Sir Robert the Doctor looked back penitently at the perspiring policeman. 'Thank you very much for your co-operation, Sergeant,' he said disarmingly. The officer of the law fell back, relieved and exonerated.

'What's going on?' asked Sir Robert.

'He wants to stop at Cranleigh Halt, Sir Robert,' replied the Sergeant.

'Why?' demanded the Chief Constable with bleak suspicion.

'I'd like to show you my credentials,' said the Doctor.

'Credentials?'

'I'd like to offer you proof of my identity.'

'At Cranleigh Halt? At a railway station?'

'My time-machine is there.'

Ah, that was it! H. G. Wells again. *The Time-Machine, The Man Who Could Work Miracles, The War Of The Worlds.* All that rubbish! That futuristic nonsense! Sir Robert looked at the Doctor's flushed and open face. It was less and less the face of a murderer, but what about that of a madman? It could be said in some quarters that this fellow played cricket like a madman. He'd beaten Percy Fender's record. That had been sheer genius. And hadn't he read somewhere that genius and madness went hand in hand?

'Please,' went on the Doctor. 'It's not out of your way, is it?'

'No.'

'Then please!'

Sir Robert made up his mind. He looked back at Sergeant Markham and opened the door of the car. 'All right, Sergeant, you carry on. The Doctor will ride with me.'

The Sergeant saluted and made himself scarce, glad to be rid of the responsibility. Sir Robert watched the Doctor closely as he joined him in the back of the Rolls: the wide, wide smile and the manic eyes. Yes, he would do well to humour the man and to have him nearer to hand.

Both cars pulled into the forecourt of Cranleigh Halt railway station. The Doctor's companions spilled from the Morris-Cowley and shot to the Rolls like iron filings sucked to a magnet. Sir Robert descended from the regally elevated back seat followed by the Doctor who looked urbanely at the cluster of eager faces anxious for the comforting cocoon of the TARDIS. The corpulent Markham panted up to Sir Robert awaiting orders, but it was the Doctor who spoke: 'You lot don't need to come. You stay here with the Sergeant.'

'Don't need to . . .' Tegan's words trailed to nothing from a gaping mouth.

'No,' went on the Doctor. 'I just want to show Sir Robert, that's all. You'll only be in the way.'

'In the way?' echoed Adric.

'Yes,' insisted the Doctor, nursing a swelling feeling that time was of the essence. 'You stay here with the Sergeant.'

The Doctor had to consider that any explanation of the TARDIS in the year 1925 would be very heavy going. To begin with, the systems of quantum mechanics and relativity had been officially accepted only a matter of five years earlier and were certainly not generally known. He was by no means certain that he could persuade the intellectually sheltered Sir Robert that the TARDIS was not the work of an apprentice sorcerer but the predictably superstitious reaction of

Sergeant Markham must certainly influence the Chief Constable and time was running out. He eyed the truculent faces of his companions. 'You three stay here with the Sergeant.' He turned to Sir Robert. 'It's on the platform.'

'What is?'

'What I have to show you.'

Tegan irately watched the Doctor lead Sir Robert through the wicket gate to the platform and marched purposefully after them. Adric and Nyssa held back not because they were more apprehensive of the Doctor's wrath than Tegan but because they had more faith that he knew what he was doing. Unlike Tegan they shared galactic experience with the Doctor: a sort of metaphysical mother's milk.

The Doctor stared incredulously at an empty platform and then hurriedly looked about him. The TARDIS was nowhere to be seen.

'Well?' prompted Sir Robert.

'It's gone,' said the Doctor hollowly.

'What has?'

'What I was going to show you.'

'Oh!' fumed Tegan and stamped her foot. The bemused Doctor allowed himself to be led back to the Rolls and gently prodded into it. Sir Robert instructed the young constable to abandon his seat by the chauffeur and join him in the back with Hathaway and the Doctor. This madman was, after all, accused of a crime of violence. It was only sensible to take proper precautions. There was safety in numbers.

Dittar Latoni mounted to the landing outside the door of the tower room and listened carefully for a moment before inserting the key in the lock. He opened the door quietly, with watchful eyes on the bed and its still unconscious occupant. He closed and locked the door behind him, pocketed the key, and advanced on the bed. He stared down for a moment at the gruesome, sleeping face, its excesses now masked in shadow, and then sat on the bed.

'Ah, my friend, my good friend,' he whispered. 'How I wish we were back on the river together ... the long river which is the only lasting peace.'

Latoni rose from the bed and looked at the barred twilight window. The moon would not be full again tonight. The danger was past. He moved to the desk and switched on the lamp throwing new shadows across the sleeping creature. He sat at the desk and opened his book. The eye in the face on the bed opened slowly and focussed in the light from the lamp on the reading Indian.

'And knowing all this, you let Robert take them away?'

The dowager Marchioness of Cranleigh avoided looking at her son. She sat in the darkening drawing room, her face turned from his angry voice, watching the servants clear the terrace of evidence of the abandoned fancy dress ball. 'Mother, that's downright wicked!'

Lady Cranleigh's back stiffened at the accusation. 'You've no right to use that word,' she said quietly. 'It's a question of moral obligation.'

'There's nothing moral about it. This man ... this Doctor whoever he is ... is innocent, and so are his friends.'

'It's because he's innocent he won't suffer. I'm surprised you can't see that.'

'Won't suffer? With all the evidence piled against him ... and with him living in this fantasy world of his? He won't stand a chance, and you know it.'

'I know that in this country a man can't be convicted on circumstantial evidence alone.'

Cranleigh moved away from his mother, pacing the room agitatedly and trying to keep his voice from rising. 'Not on circumstantial evidence alone, but without an alternative suspect there can't be any benefit of doubt, don't you see?'

'No, I don't see. What I *do* see is that we have our duty to perform.'

'Duty! Mother, we can't go on like this. We mustn't.'

'Mustn't!' Lady Cranleigh's tone was dangerous.

'Mustn't! What about Ann? Have you thought of her?'

Lady Cranleigh didn't answer at once. She turned to look at her son long and hard. 'How can you possibly ask me that?'

'But I *do* ask that! What will happen to her when she finds out?'

'She won't find out.'

'But she must! Mother, two murders have been committed, the male nurse and James. That's got to come out.'

'No. Robert will see that it doesn't.'

The statement stopped Cranleigh in his tracks. He looked at his mother in wonderment. Could she be holding something back? Had she some special knowledge of this whole miserable affair that had been withheld from him?

'Robert will? How?'

'I will speak to him.'

'Speak to him?' Cranleigh was aghast. 'Mother, Robert is a public servant. He can't ignore two murders.'

'Accidents.'

'Call it what you like, two men have died.'

'Charles, we're not without influence or friends in the county. When Robert hears of our suffering he will know where his duty lies.'

Cranleigh was silent for a moment. He turned away to the windows and watched the servants at work on the terrace. 'And what of Ann's suffering?' he asked quietly.

'Ann will not know.'

'Ann must be told.'

'*No!*'

Cranleigh turned from the window to look at his mother. He moved with slow deliberation to sit on the sofa next to her. When he spoke his voice was little above a whisper. 'Mother, if we don't tell Ann ... and she finds out ... she'll never forgive us. You know that, don't you?'

Lady Cranleigh was silent, looking sightlessly at the ever-lengthening shadows on the lawns beyond the terrace until the doors from the hall clicked open and a small voice from behind her said, 'Charles, please don't leave me alone.'

'Ann!' Cranleigh rose and went to her, gathering her into the room and securing the doors behind her. 'Ann, there's something you've got to know.'

Lady Cranleigh stood to her full height. 'No, Charles, no!'

'Yes, mother!'

The constable on duty at the reception counter looked up as the station door opened. With good reason he didn't immediately recognise the grandiose gentleman from the eighteenth century who entered ahead of four other strangely assorted characters and Sergeant Markham.

'Right!' rapped Sir Robert. 'Let's get on with it!'

'Yes, Sir Robert,' responded the Sergeant. 'Cummings, the charge book!'

Constable Cummings fumbled for the charge book beneath the counter top and took professional stock of the four unfamiliar, mournful faces before him. From the way these felons were dressed they had been apprenhended for being up to no good at Cranleigh Hall. He opened the book and began laboriously to pen the heading, *Drunk And Disorderly*, speaking as he wrote. 'Did you see it, Sarge?'

'Did I see what?'

'That thing in the yard.'

'What thing?'

'Well, it says it's a police box, but it's not like anything I've ever seen before.'

The Doctor closed his eyes and heaved a great sigh of relief. The news even brought something resembling smiles to the unhappy faces of his companions. Constable Cummings droned on as he dredged a way across the page with his pen.

'No, of course. You were over Chiddleton way. It was on the eastbound platform at the Halt. Nobody knows how it got there. And it's as heavy as lead. Had to call the Army in over at Crowshott. And we can't get into it. No key'll unlock it.'

'This one will,' said the Doctor and dipped into a pocket to produce the key of the TARDIS which he held up delicately between finger and thumb. 'With your permission, Sir Robert, this is what I wanted to show you. Perhaps you'll lead the way, Sergeant.'

Markham looked at Sir Robert who answered him with a nod of affirmation and the Sergeant led the way through the station to the yard at the back. There stood the TARDIS: faded, battered, woebegone, but totally reassuring. The Doctor stepped briskly forward, used the key and moved aside with a courtly gesture, inviting Sir Robert to enter. The Chief Constable disappeared into the TARDIS and the Doctor turned to Markham. 'You next, Sergeant.'

'There won't be any room,' complained the portly policeman.

'You *are* in for a surprise,' cooed Tegan with a great beam of undiluted pleasure.

9

The Secret of Cranleigh Hall

The sky beyond the barred window was darker now and the trees full of roosting rooks.

With infinite caution and imperceptible movement the creature on the bed, its wide eye fixed on Latoni, had moved itself onto its side. The Indian, deep in his book, was unsuspecting of the inch by inch progress of the creature easing its legs from the bed to the floor, the infinitesimal sound covered by the not so distant birds saluting the coming of night.

As Latoni turned a page the creature stood stock-still and waited for the Indian to become absorbed once more before continuing the forward creep with atavistic stealth. Nearer and nearer crept the creature, led by the ardent concentration in the single inflamed eye that burned red in the light of the lamp. One monstrous hand was now slowly extending, leading the arm to a position that would place it swiftly under the chin of the victim, dragging back the head.

Latoni turned another page but, this time, the creature did not pause. With creative cunning it used the sound and the movement to cover the remaining distance with the speed of a striking snake. Latoni was dragged choking from the chair and clawing at the nerveless arm that denied breath to his bursting lungs. His frenetic use of heels and elbows to free himself from the merciless grip robbed him of what oxygen remained. In his last seconds of consciousness the Indian groped for the key in his pocket and flung his weight to one side, toppling both himself and his assailant to the floor. Before the world became black his fingers found a space between the floor boards into which he stuffed the key.

*

Sir Robert Muir, Lord Lieutenant of the county and its Chief Constable, was at a complete loss. So much so that he had but half listened to the Doctor's learned explanation of another 'dimension' and the mnemonic Time And Relative Dimensions In Space. He looked round the control room of the TARDIS in extended awe at the incredible space and the unimaginable materials, reminding himself continually that this couldn't be a dream because the experience was shared with that dolt Markham whose gaping eyes and open mouth were beginning to get on his nerves. Couldn't the man's mentality grasp an abstract context? Hadn't he listened to the Doctor? What was that line from the play he'd done at Eton ...? ... *there are more things in heaven and earth, Horatio* ... etcetera ... etcetera ...

He looked round at the happily smiling faces of the Doctor's companions. If these ... children ... could accept the extraordinary, surely that well-fed, middle-aged policeman could come to terms with it. He'd shut that silly open mouth in the name of the county constabulary. 'Unbelievable!' he said enthusiastically. 'Unbelievable!'

'Would you like to see the Cloisters?' asked Nyssa.

'Cloisters!'

'Through this way,' indicated Nyssa.

'Well, come on, Markham!' said Sir Robert testily.

The mangled hands ran yet again over Latoni's inert body, seeking the key to the door the creature knew the Indian to possess. Grunting with frustration, the creature abandoned the insensible body of its custodian and began to ransack the desk, pulling out all the drawers and scattering their contents about the room.

The inflamed eye focussed on a box of matches, considering it at length. Then the crippled hands began a sustained attack on the books, sweeping the contents of the well-stocked shelves to the floor and ripping out the pages for them to be crumpled to tinder and thrust against the bottom of the door. This was joined by a great pile of splayed volumes before the fettered fingers fumbled to separate a match from the box to take tenuous hold of it. The match flared and the flame was touched to the crushed paper at the base of the door. Within seconds the dust-dry material was fiercely alight.

Ann Talbot sat staring into a void, experiencing a numbness that was as intolerable as the shock and pain that had preceded it. What she had been told beggared belief. She had been thrust into a nightmare world inconceivable and incomprehensible to those whose social conscience had been formed in the calm climate of accepted standards of civilised behaviour. Her whole body began to tremble violently and uncontrollably. Lady Cranleigh moved in quickly and sat beside her on the sofa.

'Don't touch me!' Ann managed to mumble. 'Don't even come near me!'

Lady Cranleigh turned to look at her son, the hurt eyes fixed in accusation. Cranleigh returned the look unflinchingly. 'She had to be told, mother,' he said quietly.

He went down on one knee before the shaking girl who shrank from him as if from defilement. 'Ann, my dear,' he went on gently. 'I had to tell you, I had to. It would have been wicked for you to have found out in any other way.'

'Wicked?' the girl whispered. And then: 'All this time. All this time.'

'I'm truly terribly sorry,' said Cranleigh, 'that it had to come to this. We acted for the best, mother and me. And up until today it was for the best. You must believe that. When you've had time to think you'll come to believe it.'

'Time to think,' echoed the stricken girl.

Cranleigh rose to his feet and crossed to the doors. 'And now I'm going to telephone the police.' Lady Cranleigh got up quickly. 'No, mother! Nothing you can say is going to stop me. Nothing! And I'm convinced that when people know the truth they will understand. They will see that no one can be blamed for all this.'

*

Tegan and Adric watched the Doctor busy at the control console.

'All right,' Tegan said. 'Where to now?'

'Cranleigh Hall,' answered the Doctor.

'We're not going back there!' protested Adric.

'Yes,' confirmed the Doctor.

'Why?' asked Tegan.

'Let's call it unfinished business.'

'If you ask me, we're the business. And if we go back there we'll certainly be finished.'

'But I'm not asking you,' said the Doctor pointedly.

Nyssa came back from the relative regions of the TARDIS followed by the two concussed representatives of the county constabulary.

'Well,' said Sir Robert mechanically. And again, 'Well!'

Tegan and Nyssa exchanged a mischievous smirk. The Chief Constable joined the Doctor and cast a confused eye over the complex circuitry of the control console. 'This is all going to look very complicated in my report.'

'Adric will give you a hand,' said the Doctor blithely. 'He's the physicist among us.'

Sir Robert looked askance at the youth who was still, he suspected, simply saturated behind the ears. Entrust a child to a senior officer's report? 'And now,' continued the Doctor, 'now that I've shown you my credentials, so to speak. I'd like you to accompany me back to Cranleigh Hall.'

'Back to the Hall?'

'With a rather more open mind,' admonished the Doctor gently.

Sir Robert considered this carefully. This Doctor-who-ever-he-was clearly enjoyed great power and was possessed of prodigious intellect for all his eccentricity and the apparent magic of his H. G. Wells machine. It was also clear that he had considerable integrity suggesting, as he was, that he be returned to the scene of the crime of which he was suspected. The man was either innocent or a master criminal. He turned to the muddled Markham. 'Hear that, Sergeant? An open mind.'

As if in answer, two dull thuds reverberated through the

TARDIS, the second following quickly on the first. The Doctor knew the sound instantly for what it was and activated the scanner. The screen showed a perplexed Police Constable Cummings who tapped again on the door of the TARDIS and bleated, 'Anybody about?'

Sir Robert and Sergeant Markham were again transfixed with amazement at yet another demonstration of a technology far beyond their comprehension. The Doctor smote the red knob on the console and called, 'Come in!'

Cummings entered the TARDIS tentatively, expecting to have to stand shoulder to shoulder with other occupants in the dark. He squinted in superstitious terror at what he beheld and squeaked, 'Strike me pink!' His stupefaction wandered from the general to the particular, to the six human beings lost in the vastness of the police box interior.

'Pull yourself together, Cummings!' said Markham importantly. 'What is it?'

'A c–c–c–' stuttered the goggle-eyed policeman.

'Come on, man!' ordered the superior Sergeant.

'A c-call from Lord C-Cranleigh, Sarge. Up at the Hall. There's another body been found. A servant called Digby. And he wants to see Sir Robert. Lord Cranleigh, I mean . . . wants to see Sir Robert.'

The Doctor and the Chief Constable looked at each other, the latter already framing a mental apology. 'The body in the cupboard?' he asked.

'Without a doubt,' replied the Doctor. 'Which is why I'd like to return with you. I think you'll find that someone took advantage of my temporary absence from my room and borrowed my fancy dress costume. Certain things were then performed in it for which I've been blamed.'

Even Sir Robert Muir's many critics couldn't accuse him of not taking things in his stride. On this occasion he strode for the door of the TARDIS. 'Come along, then, Doctor,' he said.

The Doctor held up a hand. 'If you've no objection to accompanying me, Sir Robert,' he said, 'I can get you there much quicker.' Sir Robert's recent experience, albeit confused, gave him no reason for contradicting the claim.

'Very well,' he said.

The Doctor eased the dumbfounded police constable to the door. 'Please, Mr Cummings, if you don't mind.'

The chair crashed through the glass of the barred window and the creature craned upwards to gulp in the smoke-free air. Grunting in relief it looked back towards the blazing door and held up the seat of the chair in an ineffectual attempt to shield itself from the intense heat. Holding the chair in front of it the creature advanced towards the door and stooped to lay hold of Latoni. It dragged the Indian away from the creeping flames towards the bed from which it tugged a blanket to baffle the smoke. The creature rushed back to the chair, lifted it high and began to pound at the burning door to the accompaniment of clicking, guttural cries.

At the third blow the smouldering door began to shatter and, very soon, was sufficiently breached for the creature to escape. The rush of air from the landing thinned the smoke in the room but further fed the flames. The creature threw aside the chair and turned to scoop up Latoni. As one, they smashed through the door to the landing beyond and stumbled down the steps to the corridor of the secret annexe.

When Cranleigh came back from the study Ann was still where he'd left her, hunched on the sofa, withdrawn, remote from Lady Cranleigh who was at the windows looking out on the empty lawns in the frowning twilight. 'The police are on their way,' he said. He looked at his mother's unresponsive back for a moment. 'I'll meet them if you'd like to go and change.'

His mother turned to face him. 'I've never flinched from my duty,' she said quietly, 'and I shall not now.'

Anger suddenly lighted Ann's dull eyes. She struggled to her feet incensed by the older woman's obvious pride in the unspeakable horror to which she'd just confessed. 'How could you!' she cried. 'Oh, how could you!' She ran to the doors, wrenched them open and fled across the hall.

She didn't see the creature limping down the stairs supporting the unconscious Latoni on his shoulders but Cranleigh, in pursuit of her, did. The creature stopped before it reached the foot of the stairs and Cranleigh faced it, half crouching, as if waiting for a wild animal to spring.

'All right, old chap,' he breathed. 'All right.'

The TARDIS materialised on the main driveway of Cranleigh Hall not fifty yards from the entrance. The Doctor was the first to emerge followed closely by Sir Robert and the others. Ann ran blindly from the Hall and raced down the driveway towards the TARDIS and its passengers. Seeing her distress, Sir Robert took her instantly into his arms.

Sensing danger, the Doctor hurried on to the Hall, followed by his companions and the labouring Markham. The great front doors stood open and the Doctor was first through them to see Cranleigh and the creature still facing each other. Cranleigh took no notice of the Doctor's arrival but lifted his hands to the creature demonstrating that he meant no harm. 'All right, old chap,' he whispered again. 'Nobody's going to hurt you.'

The Doctor heard sharp intakes of breath from his companions and a blasphemous expression of horror from the Sergeant at the sight of what faced them on the stairs. Suddenly everything fell into place for the Doctor. All the questions that had tormented him were answered at a stroke.

The creature on the stairs, still burdened with the Indian, had been the part missing from the composite, but now that this part had come to light the whole picture could be understood. Such monstrous deformity was no accident of birth; this disfigurement was man-made. Certain tribes of Indian in the rain forests of South America (explored by the ninth Marquess of Cranleigh) perpetrated such bestialities, visiting on their victims the demands of vengeful gods. A terrible irony, thought the Doctor, that most of man's inhumanity to man was at the invocation of jealous gods in all their many seductive guises.

This mutilated victim, cared for in comfort and in secret,

was no stranger to the Cranleigh household. This mockery of God's image crouched so grotesquely on the stairs had to be held in high regard by the woman who had perjured herself so shamelessly to protect him. Both reason and instinct told the Doctor that the creature on the stairs was none other then George Beauchamp, ninth Marquess of Cranleigh.

It was a deduction confirmed by the dowager Marchioness who now stood at the open doors to the drawing room. 'George,' she said quietly. 'No, George.' It was the unmistakable tone of a mother rebuking a son. It drew a gasp from Nyssa who clutched at Tegan's arm. George's inflamed eye had taken in the alert Doctor, his tense younger brother, the gawping Sergeant, and his mother, statuesque in her private hell, her public agony. The eye now concentrated on Nyssa.

Slowly the ninth Marquess shifted the weight of Latoni from his shoulders and allowed the Indian to slip to the stair treads. Anticipating his brother's intention, Cranleigh stepped into his path as he advanced from the stairs. A lumpen hand swept up from inertia like the thong of a whip and sent the younger brother sprawling. Adric, nearer Nyssa and quicker off the mark than the Doctor, sprang to the girl's defence, only to be lifted clear of the floor by the monstrous and maniacal arms and hurled at the lunging Doctor. A mitten-like hand clamped on Nyssa's slender arm and she was dragged, screaming, to the stairs. As Markham lumbered to the rescue George secured the fragile girl about the waist and used the other deformed extremity to threaten her throat. From the floor Cranleigh thrust out an arm.

'No, Sergeant! Get back! He's killed twice!'

Nyssa's voice gurgled to a breathless choking at the onset of revulsion and horror as she was borne inexorably up the stairs from the top of which eddies of smoke now appeared. Disregarding Cranleigh, the Doctor leapt to the stairs. 'No, Doctor!' cried Lady Cranleigh. 'He'll not harm her. He thinks she's Ann.'

The Doctor turned back. 'And when he finds she's not?'

'He won't. My son is out of his mind. Dittar, here, is the only one who can influence him.'

Cranleigh had moved to examine the unconscious Indian.

'An influence we've no time to wait for!' called back the Doctor as he bounded up the stairs into the thickening smoke. Cranleigh straightened from his examination of Latoni.

'He'll be all right, but get him outside!' He rushed up the stairs hard on the heels of the Doctor yelling, 'Get everybody outside and telephone the fire brigade.' He, too, disappeared into the smoke as Markham lumbered towards a telephone and Adric and Tegan began to tug Latoni to safety. Lady Cranleigh closed her eyes and her lips began to move in silent prayer.

When the Doctor reached the second floor Cranleigh was behind him. Both breathed through handkerchiefs clamped over nose and mouth, leaving blinking eyes to smart painfully. The wall containing the main secret panel had already surrendered to the greedily licking tongues of flame.

'It's no use,' came the muffled voice of Cranleigh. 'It's got too much of a hold.' But the Doctor was not to be stopped. Nyssa was in dreadful danger and neither fire nor high water would hold back the Doctor. He raced through the smoke to his room. 'No, Doctor!' called Cranleigh, before he was forced back to the head of the stairs. His mother was still standing where he'd left her when he regained the hall.

'Outside, mother!' he said firmly.

'The servants must be warned,' was all she replied, with a quiet calm.

'I'll do that.'

He took her by the elbow and began to steer her towards the entrance doors as Markham came from the study. 'Sergeant, may I ask you to look after my mother?'

'Yes, milord,' was the ready response.

'I'm perfectly capable of looking after myself, Sergeant,' said Lady Cranleigh succinctly, detaching herself from her son. She walked erect and without haste to the entrance of the Hall, respectfully followed by Markham, as Cranleigh made his way swiftly to the back stairs.

*

The Doctor had gambled on the maxim that fortune favours the brave and hoped that it extended to the foolhardy. He was not disappointed. In his room the secret panel eventually yielded to his probing fingers and the door pivoted open, but this time he took the precaution of wedging it open with the bedspread before venturing into the recess between the walls. He remembered the exact position of the opposing panel and was soon in the parallel corridor already redolent of incipient fumes. In a moment he was at the end of the corridor and stamping on the floor of the cupboard. As the back slid aside he had again to defend himself with the handkerchief against the billowing smoke. The heat from the blaze at the far end of the corridor was as from a furnace and long tongues of flame, which had already engulfed the bathroom, were fast feeling their way along the floor and both walls.

A table had been dragged from Digby's room and stood in the centre of the corridor directly under an open skylight. The Doctor climbed onto the table, reached up and took hold of the wood frame above and hauled himself to the roof.

Charles Beauchamp, no longer the tenth Marquess of Cranleigh, marshalled the last of the servants from the Hall and moved along the terrace, looking up at the pall of smoke that rose straight in the still evening air. He ran to the wall beyond the windows and began to climb the thick stems of the centuries-old ivy. Adric rushed to follow his example but the not over-agile Markham was quick to hold him back.

'No, lad, not you!'

Tegan took over from the Sergeant with an arm round the boy which suggested she was more in need of his support than the climbing nobleman. Lady Cranleigh watched her younger son reach beyond the level of the first floor windows and then walked with dignity to where Sir Robert still comforted the distraught Ann. 'Robert, I've done something terribly wrong,' she said simply.

'I know,' he responded with a glance at Ann. 'But why, Madge, why?'

'It was the black orchid. To the Butiu Indians it's sacred.

They cut out his tongue and hung him by the heels over a very slow fire. It was done every day for a week.' She looked at Latoni, now recovered and kneeling on the grass in prayer. 'There's the man who rescued him. Dittar thinks George was insane from the first hour. It would have been more merciful to let him die.'

Sir Robert had let the suffering woman finish but he now repeated his question. 'Why here?'

'Oh, Robert! Mindless? Misshapen? Locked up, without care, in a loveless institution?' The tears came freely now but the head was still held high. Ann slowly detached herself from Sir Robert and came forward to offer her arms. The two women combined in a fierce embrace.

'The blame's all mine,' said Lady Cranleigh softly. 'I should never have insisted on engaging the male nurse. Poor, poor fellow. But Dittar was becoming ill with coping single-handed. There has to be some limit to devotion.'

'No! Don't blame yourself!' whispered Ann. 'Don't blame yourself!

'*There!*'

The shout was from Henry, the footman, pointing upwards. The ninth Marquess appeared beyond a low parapet at the edge of the roof one arm locked about Nyssa and the other flailing at the smouldering hem of her dress. The younger brother halted his climb just short of the roof and tried to gauge from the pointing below where his quarry might be.

The Doctor, following the only path possible for Nyssa's captor, had fetched up behind a chimney stack from where, unseen, he could watch George's progress along the parapet. From here he saw Charles climb onto the roof some twelve feet beyond his brother and saw him hold out a hand pleadingly.

'George! Please, George!'

George stopped with a suddenness which almost toppled him. There was a gasp from the watchers below, repeated as Nyssa was held deliberately close to the edge. Nyssa, terror-stricken to the point of inertia, screamed as she saw the terrace beneath her. The sound of Charles's voice and the resurgence of hope of rescue made her renew the pummelling and scratching at the nerveless, shapeless head and shoulders. Charles held his ground, not daring to risk aid to the threatened Nyssa.

'George. She's done you no harm.'

The Doctor came out quickly from the shelter of the stack and found foot and finger holds in the wall beneath the level of the parapet. Slowly but surely he forced his way along the wall to find a vantage point to the rear of the deranged man and his hysterical hostage. Within six feet of them he heaved himself onto the parapet and said as quietly as his pounding pulses would let him. 'Be still, Nyssa!'

George whirled on the Doctor and Nyssa screamed again, feeling herself flung to the very edge. Charles jumped to the advantage of the distraction but the insane lack no cunning. George used Nyssa like a flail and her feet took Charles full in the face. The younger brother went down like a sack and wedged in the narrow gulley between the parapet and the steeply rising tiles of the roof.

George turned back to the Doctor and opened his mouth in a ghastly, toothless, welcoming smile of triumph.

The Doctor gambled again. He had put more pieces of the picture together. The Beauchamp brothers had been rivals for the hand of Ann Talbot and the older had won her. Won her, only to lose her again in circumstances of unimaginable horror. The arrival of Nyssa on this tragic scene had given the tormented man a double image of his lost love and had proved intolerable to his fevered mind. It was transparently clear that if George was denied Ann, Charles would be also.

The Doctor was close enough to the now more controlled Nyssa to reach out a hand and touch her, but he restrained himself. He looked directly, searchingly, into the inflamed eye.

'Lord Cranleigh,' he said gently, 'that isn't Miss Talbot. Miss Talbot is down there. Look!'

The red eye looked down at the people grouped below, searching among them in the fading light. Ann stepped forward, separating herself from those about her. The eye lingered on the distant girl and then moved to refocus on Nyssa whose eyes returned the look in abject terror. George lifted his mangled hand from which Nyssa shrank. Gently he moved the shoulder strap of her dress. There was no mole.

'Lord Cranleigh,' went on the Doctor as before, 'you are a man of science and a man of honour whose skill and courage are already legend. I beg you, sir, to do nothing that will change the memory of you in the minds of your many admirers the world over.'

The eye turned from the fainting Nyssa to search out the Doctor's face. For those on the ground the suspense reduced breathing to the bare minimum. The only sounds to break in on the unearthly silence came from the voracious appetite of the lengthening flames and the bell of a faraway fire engine. Then what remained of a once noble head lifted in dignity and George Beauchamp, ninth Marquess of Cranleigh, held out Nyssa to the waiting arms of the Doctor.

The sigh of relief that rose from below was suddenly stifled as the unburdened nobleman stepped up onto the parapet and held out his empty arms to Ann down below.

'George, no!' shouted his brother.

George jerked towards the sound, lost his balance, and plummeted to the terrace.

Nyssa smothered her face and her feelings in the Doctor's breast and Charles forced himself back onto his feet. Below on the terrace the shocked group watched Sir Robert and Markham stoop by the body.

A weeping Tegan was clumsily comforted by Adric whose grief at what had happened was expressed in embarrassment at the quality of the suffering he saw all about him. He looked in open admiration at the controlled Lady Cranleigh as she accepted the sad shaking of Sir Robert's head as confirmation of the death of the son she had protected from a cruel world for two long, arduous years.

Upon the roof the Doctor held out his hand to the dead man's brother and it was taken warmly, gratefully.

'I'm so deeply sorry, Doctor. What must you think of us?'

'It's not for me to make such judgements,' murmured the Doctor. 'But for the grace of God there goes any of us.'

Epilogue

Three days later the Doctor and his companions stood by the TARDIS as they prepared to bid farewell to Cranleigh Hall. The public response to the truth about George Beauchamp, botanist and explorer, had been overwhelming, the deaths of two innocent men being indirectly attributed to the barbaric depths of the South American rain forests: the barbaric depths of man's inhumanity to man, thought the Doctor.

'Thank you all for staying for the funeral,' said Lady Cranleigh, a statement endorsed by her younger son and his fiancée with nods and smiles, for all the words had been said. 'And we'd like you to have this.'

The Doctor took the Morocco-bound book from her extended hand and opened it. On the fly leaf was a print of the portrait that hung at the Hall: the author as he was before his fateful return to the Orinoco. The title page read:

BLACK ORCHID
an exploration
by
George Beauchamp

The Doctor closed the book, much moved. 'Thank you,' he said simply. 'It will be treasured always.' And he doffed his hat and followed his companions into the TARDIS.

THIS OFFER EXCLUSIVE TO

READERS

Pin up magnificent full colour posters of DOCTOR WHO

Just send £2.50 for the first poster and £1.25 for each additional poster

TO: PUBLICITY DEPARTMENT
W. H. ALLEN & CO PLC
44 HILL STREET
LONDON W1X 8LB

Cheques, Postal Orders made payable to WH Allen PLC

POSTER 1 ☐   POSTER 2 ☐   POSTER 3 ☐
POSTER 4 ☐   POSTER 5 ☐

Please allow 28 DAYS for delivery.

I enclose £ _____

CHEQUE NO. _____

ACCESS, VISA CARD NO. _____

Name _____

Address _____

_____

_____

*For Australia, New Zealand, USA and Canada apply to distributors listed on back cover for details and local price list